Wartime Tales: The Taming of the Snoek and Other Stories

An Anthology by Various Authors

First published by
Scott Martin Productions, 2019
www.scottmartinproductions.com

Various Authors

First published in Great Britain in 2019 by
Scott Martin Productions
10 Chester Place,
Adlington, Chorley, PR6 9RP
scottmartinproductions@gmail.com
www.scottmartinproductions.com

Electronic and paperback versions available for purchase on Amazon.
Copyright (c) Lesley Atherton

All rights reserved. Without limiting the rights under copyright reserved above, no part of this publication may be reproduced, stored or introduced into a retrieval system, or transmitted, in any form or by any means (electronic, mechanical, photocopying, recording or otherwise), without the prior written permission of both the copyright owner and the publisher of this book.

Huge thanks to Morrigan Atherton-Forshaw for this original cover art on this publication. Her piece is titled 'Behind Each Man' and was the 11-14 age group winner of the Never Such Innocence art competition, 2018.

Contents

The Telegram: A True Story *by Mary Newsham* 4
The Taming of the Snoek *by Lesley Atherton* 15
Bug Out *by Denis Kirkham* 21
Hero? Not from where I'm standing! *by Delia Southern* ... 41
A Soldier's Prayer *by Sally James* 42
A Pantoum About the Somme July 1st 1916 *by Sally James* 44
Death Day *by Denis Kirkham* 45
Futility *by Sally James* 52
Raindrop *by Eva Korwin-Szymanowska* 53
May Day *by Eva Korwin-Szymanowska* 56
Home Coming *by Denis Kirkham* 58
Brown Envelope *by Denis Kirkham* 62
The Officer *by Denis Kirkham* 64
Preparing for Christmas, 1944 *by Delia Southern* 68
Daphne Alone *by Lesley Atherton* 70
Last Post *by Sally James* 73
In the Trench *by Delia Southern* 74
War: The Fallen: Honoured and Spurned *by Peter Hull* ... 75
Room For One More *by Neville Southern* 78
Isabel's Kitchen *by Delia Southern* 79
Publisher and Other Publications 81
2018 titles 81
2019 titles (confirmed) 82

The Telegram: A True Story
by Mary Newsham

'Come on mum, we're going to be late,' called Mick, impatiently waiting in the street while his younger brother stood quietly, in a world of his own, rolling marbles along the slanted top of the garden wall. He wanted to see how far along he could get them to go before they fell off.

Lily was late as usual. Swinging into her coat she slammed the front door a little too hard. As a smiling postman pushed past the boys into the small front garden, he thrust a telegram into her hand saying cheerily, 'I hope it's not bad news love'.

Lily tore open the envelope as Mick grabbed at her arm and pulled at her, urging her on. She tried reading as they hurried down the road but all she could make out was the army number of her husband followed by his full name. The rest didn't make any sense to her. She stopped to read again, as if that would make it clearer than reading on the move, but still she didn't understand.

Lily decided that she would get the boys into school first, so she'd quickened her pace. Mick eagerly rushed through the school gates and dashed off to find his mates. Lily, instead of following the boys in as she usually did, called out to the bemused group of mums that she often chatted with.

'I can't stop. I have something urgent to do,' she said, and without waiting for a reply hurried back in the direction she'd come from.

Turning into a side road two before her own Lily sped along towards the corner shop that her mother ran at the far end of the street. Lily burst in through the narrow double doors, stunning the gently gossiping shoppers into silence. Waving the small piece of paper in the air she cried, 'Look mum… look what I have got… a telegram!'

'What does it say?' urged Ellen from behind the counter.

'I don't know; I don't understand it,' stammered Lily adding. 'It's got something to do with Bert.'

The group parted like a biblical sea to let Ellen through to her daughter. She took the telegram and read it for herself. As she did, the little group of shoppers re-congregated around but behind her, peering over her shoulders to see for themselves the mysterious message.

Lily asked her mother: 'What does it say? Do you understand it?'

Ellen, unlike her daughter, did not recognise the army number, but could read the name of her gentle son-in law who was so perfectly matched with her chaotic daughter. She answered forlornly, 'No, I don't. It's obviously about Bert, but that's all I can tell'.

The soft, background murmurings now expanded into haphazard questioning without the expectation of any reply. That, in turn, quickly changed into an increasing crescendo of suggestions and ideas as to the note's meaning. The clamour unexpectedly halted when one of the most unassuming of customers raised her voice and announced in an unquestionable manner, 'Well, it's in French, isn't it!'

There was another stunned silence, broken when one voice gingerly questioned 'How do you know?'

The young woman explained. 'My sister married a Frenchman and has been learning the language.'

Before she was allowed to continue, seeing a glimmer of hope, another voice broke in. 'Can you read it then?'

'No,' she replied quickly. 'When my sister writes to me she adds little bits of the language she has learned in the hopes that I will learn some. I recognise some of it, but I don't know what means.'

'Well, will she translate it for us?' added another eager customer.

'That will take too long,' interrupted Ellen, taking charge again. 'There must be someone around here, someone local, who could help.'

Ellen, her husband and their younger children lived over the shop. The unusual sound of commotion from below had alerted Lily's sisters, who had come down to find out what was going on. Ellen set them to work serving the customers. Even though they were for the most part, now reluctant to leave, Ellen wanted them gone so that she and her daughter could work out what to do.

One by one the shoppers' orders were filled and they left, each excited with the thought of helping to solve the problem of the French telegram, promising to spread the word, and ask around for anyone who could help.

Lily, realising how late she would be for work and feeling now that concentration would not be possible, began worrying about her job. Ellen gave Lily a calming cup of tea and told her she would phone the factory to explain, and that Lily must go home and remain optimistic.

But, was the telegram good news or bad?

Bert had been reported to Lily as 'missing in action' over four and a half years earlier, when defending the beaches during the evacuation of Dunkirk. She had not heard another word of his fate since. At the time he had gone to fight, she had been pregnant with their second child - another son she named Robert. He was born fit and healthy and was approaching five. He had never seen his father. Maybe never would.

Surprisingly Lily saw no-one as she walked the short distance along the lane that ran beside the railway sidings and linked the top of four parallel roads to her own home. She was sinking deep into thoughts of previous times with Bert. As she reached the house they had shared, she stood back and looked for a moment before entering and closing the door behind her. She leaned back against it, closing her eyes. It was as if, now she was on her own, she could conjure up the memories better - not only as pictures in her mind, but once again, into reality.

Lily opened her eyes and looked at the marked walls of the hall. She had two energetic sons and their friends constantly running in and out. Add to that the shortages of wartime and her having to work, and the house had become shabby.

Remembering her mother's words to be positive, Lily decided that she must try to make the best she could of their home in case Bert was to return, so she set to work cleaning.

She went into the first room along the hallway, which was the sitting room, rarely used, and kept only for special occasions or as an overflow for larger gatherings. She stood looking at the furniture, suddenly seeing as if for the first time the sagging sofa and the faded curtains. She felt the damp chill of this room, cut off and little warmed for use in this time of shortage.

Lily put on her apron, gathered what cleaning materials she had and set to work on this, the most neglected room. She circled it, dusting and polishing until she reached the now out of tune piano, and the memories flooded back of how so often she had played while friends and family stood or sat around singing. As she lifted the lid and tested the notes, the thought flashed through her mind that maybe, one day, when the war was over, it would be once again tuned and returned to its place as key voice at any sing along.

The loud rapping on the front door brought her out of

her dreams and Lily rushed to open it. There stood the local gossip Vi Mitchell. What the dickens could she want? thought Lily as she came back to reality.

'I was wondering, as I could go that way, if you wanted me to pick up the boys from school.'

Like most of the street dwellers, Vi was an acquaintance rather than a close friend, but in this time of need she was offering a friendly hand. Lily had not realised the time, so untying her apron said, 'Tell you what Vi, I'll walk down with you if you don't mind'.

She now realised that the word was out about her telegram, so having a companion who would relish fending off inquisitors could be helpful when collecting the boys from school. They were not yet aware of any of the day's activities.

Word had spread quickly and as Lily entered the school playground she was (as expected) bombarded with a barrage of questions from interested parents. True to form, Vi played her part fending off or answering the questions as she could, before having to leave to collect her own girls from the Catholic school.

Lily's boys came out of class and ran to join their mum. Several other mums approached Lily and made tentative enquiries. Finally she was encompassed by her own group of friends, who although enquiring did not press her.

A question from one of the friends finally penetrated, so following up on it, Lily approached the school office, checking as she did, that the telegram was still in her coat pocket. She knocked on the slightly open office door.

As she heard the dreaded school secretary open the door wider, she stumbled, pulling the now crumpled message from her pocket and slowly holding it out, Lily asked, 'I wonder if there is anyone here who can help?'

The secretary looked confused.

'With what?' she replied, in her brisk manner.

Lily, nervous, but knowing that this was her best chance, continued pushing the paper into her hand, 'I have received this telegram about my husband, but don't know what it says. I wonder if there is anyone here who could help?'

Mrs Christmas took the telegram and looked at it. Then after a moment's pause she announced in her sharp way, 'My husband teaches French. I can get him to translate this and return it to you in the morning, if that is of any help.' Almost ecstatic with delight, besides that fact that no other option had presented itself, Lily readily agreed.

She went back out to the playground, gathered up her two boys and set off home in a daze. She tried to do all the normal motherly things like making their tea and reading them as story before bed, but was constantly interrupted by questioning neighbours knocking on the front door.

Finally, she as tucked the boys into bed, she decided that now was the time to answer their questions about what was happening and to explain all that had gone on during this the most eventful of days. Mick, now seven and a half, had been two when his dad had left to go to war, so had very little memory of him. Bob had still not been born so knew him not at all, except from photos. How then to explain? What to explain?

Late that night, when Lily finally went to bed, she, unsurprisingly, found it impossible to sleep, so found restful contentment in the memories of times with Bert. She remembered the bicycle ride with him, his brother and his girlfriend. She had bought a new pair of the most fashionable shoes which although unsuitable for cycling she had insisted on wearing. Then it had rained and they had all got soaked through and had returned to dry off at her parent's home. In her haste she had tried to dry the shoes in the oven, with the consequence that the pointed toes had curled and stiffened, so resembling Arabian fantasy footwear. That led her to imagining them riding on a floating carpet, rather than their old bikes.

She drifted into more memories of times when they had been out on beautiful calm sunny days picnicking in the countryside.

Their wonderful wedding day. Bert looking down lovingly on his first born, Michael. He was to be known as Mick, named after Lily's own sister who although christened Mary, was such a tomboy that she was known to all as Mickey.

Lily had tried to stay positive over the years, but silence over the increasing passage of time had only served to reinforce the view that news, when it came, would be of the worst kind.

Finally exhausted from the day Lily lay in bed and listened to the familiar sounds of the softly clanging carriages as, pushed into position ready for the morning, they gently bumped each other. The soft, prolonged, relaxing hiss of the engines, letting off the steam from their boilers as they settled down for the night, soothed Lily into sleep.

Waking with a rush, not expecting or realising that she had slept and not aware of the time, Lily called the boys to get up and ready for school. The previous day's thoughts were flooding her mind as she lay breakfast on the table early. Mick and Bob were confused by their mum's readiness to be on her way to school so early.

Lily was eager to get to school this morning, but she could not explain to the boys why. A million questions flooded her mind; what if it was the worst news and Bert never returned? What if he did return, how would she...how would their boys feel about him? Bob had never even ever seen his dad, let alone known him as a person.

The boys fed, Lily hurried out of the house with them. No-one else was yet on their way, so there was no delay. She sped through the gate, left the boys in the playground and headed for the office. Frustratingly, no-one was there yet; or at least the secretary wasn't. Lily hung about the corridors until Bob called her out into the playground. The novelty of having his mum there, in the school and playground was too much.

'Look Mum, what I can do on the climbing frame,' called an excited Bob. This was a new experience. Mum was always in a rush to get off to work in the mornings. Lily watched while keeping an eye out for the secretary.

Mrs Christmas puffed heavily as she rushed across the playground.

'Where is Mrs Washington?' she asked several mothers, but none had seen her.

'Well please tell her I am in the office waiting for her,' she instructed as she headed for the buildings.

The buzz of the message on top of the mysterious telegram had permeated the playground, and soon the the news of Mrs Christmas's arrival reached Lily. She headed tremulously towards, what she hoped was the answer.

As Lily tapped on the office door the tiny secretary rushed towards her, tears in her eyes.

'Oh Lily,' she cried, grabbing her hands and unable to help herself. Pulling a sheet of paper from her handbag, she thrust it at Lily. She looked down, but before she could read the translation Mrs Christmas burst out.

'He's coming home. Your husband; he's coming home!'

Lily didn't know whether to read the paper or listen to the tearful woman in front of her.

'What!' Lily croaked, disbelieving what she had heard.

The secretary, never a demonstrative person threw her arms around Lily and cried, 'He is coming home!'

Lily flopped onto a nearby chair in total shock. Although it had been what she had always hoped for, and what she had clung onto for the last four years, now she was afraid to believe it in case it was a mistake.

Mrs Christmas, now a little calmer, pointed at the paper in Lily's hand and said 'Read it. My husband translated it last night. I tried to get here early but the buses are having problems. It says that he's coming home within forty eight hours of receiving this telegram!'

Lily unable to move out of the chair, must have read it twenty times by the time the diminutive secretary came back with a cup of tea. She looked up in shock, but with realisation dawning and slowly stammered, 'That means he could be home to-day!'

Tears flowed down her face.

'Oh my goodness,' added Lily as she delved into her handbag for a hankie to wipe her nose and eyes, 'I had better get home'.

Not wishing to be rude, Lily finished the tea. She thanked Mrs Christmas and asked her to pass on her thanks to her husband, rushed out of the office and while crossing the playground, answered all questions from the entering friends and acquaintances with the same tear filled answer:

'He's coming home'.

Once again bursting into the now buzzing shop, Lily waved the page of translation, but before anyone could ask, she cried with more tears flowing, 'He's coming home; he's coming home!' This caused a stunned silence, but this time only for a very few moments before the generous customers started with offers of help.

Everyone was war-weary and although the pull-together spirit had kept people going, all were eager for good news. This was news of the very best kind and all wanted to feed from it and to be part of it.

Once again, as the true matriarch she was, Ellen took charge. Without allowing a word of protest, she ordered Lily to go home and prepare for Bert's return. She also advised that she might want to go shopping to buy, if available, at least some of his favourite foods for his first meal back.

Lily went home in a daze not knowing what to do first. She headed into their kitchen, always the family room, to try to make it as homely as possible. She hadn't been working long tidying away the boys' drawings and crayons still on the table when there was a knock at the front door. This in itself was unusual in these times when folk would knock and enter without waiting for the door to be opened for them.

Lily rushed to the door half in the expectation of an official there to apologise for a mistake in the wording of the telegram and to explain that Bert was not coming home after all. But instead, there was Vi Mitchell with a group of the local women, all in their overalls. Before Lily could ask what they wanted, Vi said 'Lily, we all want to help. Just tell us what to do and we will do it'.

Lily could not think.

This was her dream come true, so how could she share it? It couldn't possibly mean the same to them as it did to her. But these women, worn down like her by the shortages of war, were desperate to share her good news.

Before she could think or speak, Lily's eye was caught by movement in the street behind the ladies on the doorstep. She noticed that tables were being put out into the road. Pointing Lily asked the group, 'What on earth is going on here?'

Vi who had appointed herself the spokeswoman for the group answered in a much more gentle tone than was normal, 'Lily, everyone wants to celebrate your good news'. She continued, before Lily could reply, 'You have lived here for nine years. Most of us knew Bert before he went off to fight, and we all would like to celebrate; so this is a perfect excuse to have a party. Please,' she pleaded on behalf of all, 'let us do our bit to help and welcome Bert home'.

Lily was stunned by their generous offer.

'Okay. What is it you want?'

The excited clamour started at once, with most of the women voicing their own ideas.

Vi shushed them into near silence while she suggested to Lily, 'Why don't you let us clean and smarten your house, so you can go down to the shops to see what special treats you can get for Bert's return?'

Lily, never one to enjoy housework, was delighted although still somewhat bemused by this idea. So off she went, leaving the enthusiastic neighbours to it.

The butcher's shop was at the bottom of the road so it didn't take long for Lily to reach it. As usual, there were queues of patient people, chatting while waiting their turn to be served with whatever was available. Lily joined the end of the line and the lady in front of her turned to make small talk, while a few other faces turned to see who had joined them. Within a few minutes the general hubbub died down to be replaced with a new buzz of excited conversation that travelled from the front to the back of the queue.

Like Chinese whispers, the message was transferred to the last but one in the line, then, Lily found herself most unexpectedly ushered forwards and towards the counter. Feeling somewhat guilty at bypassing the patiently waiting group, Lily was confronted by the usually genial butcher asking her, 'What is your husband's favourite?'

Taken aback at the speed of her arrival at the counter and the question Lily stammered knowing that Bert's favourite had not been available for purchase during the war years, even with ration tokens.

The butcher asked again, and Lily replied without any hope, but the man disappeared out the back of the shop and reappeared with something already wrapped. Handing it to Lily he said 'I hope he enjoys this, with our compliments,' and so refused payment.

Lily left the shop, package in hand, still surprised at the speed of service, the apparent availability of the desired choice and the refusal of payment. As she wandered back towards her home, she mused over the last twenty four hours. It felt to her like she was moving in slow motion while all around her were moving at high speed - as if she was not really in touch with the real world, but occupied somewhere different. A world and time private to herself.

Half way up the road to her own home Lily became aware of commotion in the street and recognised the neighbourhood enthusiasm mounting for any excuse to celebrate.

Bunting had been strung across the road, and tables stood in rows waiting to be laden with treats. Chairs of all kinds were being brought out to put at the tables. One man had help carrying out his precious radiogram and was testing to make sure music could be heard. Some folk appeared with several bottles each of home-made wine to share.

As Lily entered her already open front door she was astonished to find the women busily cheering the walls of the hall with distemper, to the sound of music flooding in from the street, while others cleaned the stairs and kitchen or beat carpets on the line in the back garden. All was a hive of activity and so dumping her bags in the pantry, she took off her coat, put on her apron and joined in.

By mid-afternoon, when they had done the best they could, some of the women went off to collect children from school, while the rest stayed to finish what they had started.

Hearing the music and seeing the bunting and tables in the street excited the homecoming children who although unaware of the reason behind the celebrations, were immediately infected with the enthusiasm permeating the neighbourhood.

As the few men-folk and working women arrived home they too became aware of the celebration and the party atmosphere spread. People from the adjoining streets congregated, each bringing with them plates of food as plain or fancy as their own abilities allowed, and placing them on the tables for all to enjoy. People who saw each other usually only in passing now chatted like old friends, while the children played.

The air of optimism hovered like a low friendly cloud. Excitement gathered as Lily's family joined the community in the street and the singing and dancing added to the energised chatter. Ellen, having closed her shop early, went to her daughter and tapped lightly on the still open door of Lily's home as she entered.

Ellen hugged Lily, then stood back and said to her, 'Look at yourself. Do you want Bert to see you like this?'

Lily looked down at her dirty overall without answer, so Ellen continued, 'I'll go and put the kettle on'.

They stood looking at each other for what seemed a long time, then Ellen went in to the kitchen to make tea. They shared a quiet few minutes then Ellen having emptied her cup, urged Lily to go and get ready for Bert's return.

As Ellen opened the front door to leave, the mounting noise of excitement outside hit Lily and she began to believe that this was not the dream she had clung to, so dear for so long, but it really was true - her Bert was coming home, very soon.

Lily took off her apron and headed up the hallway. On the bottom stair she wondered what she should put on for Bert's return. Thinking about her clothing then realising that almost everything would look worn - if not shabby - she tried to push her wayward hair into a style. Then, as she reached the fifth step, the outside crescendo of cheering gushed in as the front door opened then faded as it closed, and she turned to see Bert.

Lily was frozen, and unable to move or say anything. She just stared. Bert, while looking at Lily motionless on the stairs, also said nothing but headed down the passage into the kitchen. Lily descended the stairs and followed a few steps behind him - still silent. Bert looked around then, spying a familiar sight, lifted the tea cosy on the still warm teapot, put his hand to it and feeling its welcoming warmth said, 'Ah, I recognise that,' then turning to her said, 'Hello gel, I'm home'.

He wrapped his arms around her as she enfolded his emaciated body in her arms and dissolved into tears.

I wrote this story when I undertook evening classes in English Language and Literature in 1990. It is my interpretation of the true story my mum told us of my dad's return home after being a prisoner of war for 4 1/2 years. He was actually listed as missing for that all that time so she did not know if he was still alive.

The Taming of the Snoek
by Lesley Atherton

As was the case with everyone in the time of conflict, Mrs Rena Armstrong had known better days. But Mrs Armstrong waxed a little more lyrical than most when it came to discussing her pet subject - food.

'It is hard enough,' she complained, with passion and conviction, 'to get hold of adequate food supplies for a common man's calorie requirements. It is even more so when your palate is discerning - as mine is'.

At this point Rena looked, pointedly, at her friend, Miss Penny Watson.

'Oh, of course,' she agreed. 'It's always been one of your interests, Rena. Everybody knows that.'

Rena, who preferred being referred to as Mrs Armstrong by her friends, always prickled slightly at being referred to as 'Rena' by Miss Watson, but, as ever, she let it slide. At least Miss Watson had an idea of what her life had been before rationing and scarcity took their toll on her pantry.

'I used to attend WI meetings, as you know, Miss Watson. Those stalwarts Mrs Katrina Smith and Mrs Olive Taylor would bring rock cakes, scones, currant buns... I would also contribute.'

'Of course you would,' agreed Penny.

'But I would add herbs and fruit and flower petals, to add piquancy and taste. Do you know that I was very politely asked to stop contributing as the flavours were too 'foreign' for their likings.'

'I'm afraid I appreciate as little as they do,' confessed Penny.

'But, of course. It matters not with you. You have only your relatively unsophisticated palate to cheer. You need only stews made with offcuts of meat, to be padded out with potatoes, and flavoured with gravy browning, salt and pepper. That is adequate, Penny dear, for your needs. But it's not enough for me, as well you know.'

Penny nodded and muffled a small sigh.

'The addition of fragranced plants and unusual herbs and vegetables is essential. It is also essential to sample new tastes. Not easy in these difficult times.'

'I can't even get enough food to stop my stomach rumbling, Rena.'

'Quite so.'

The two ladies sipped their tea quietly for a few seconds.

'Can you tell the difference between cream and mock cream, Miss Watson? Egg and powdered egg? Mackerel and snoek?'

Rena watched as Penny Watson considered the questions and huffed a little as Penny shook her head slightly.

'I'm such a dolt,' she said. 'Does it matter?'

'Not usually. Not for you. But for me it does. It's my upbringing, you see. It's what comes of being the only child of Marcel Arnette, and of being at a most impressionable age at the time when he opened the first French restaurant in this town. I learned at the apron strings of the best.'

'Yes,' agreed Penny.

'Father would daily fill a stock pot with all the restaurant's vegetable cuttings. Soup was eaten before every meal, and often was the part of the meal we enjoyed the most.'

'I remember…' began Penny.

Rena cut in.

'Before this stupid rationing, I'd regularly make fish stock from our meal's trimmings - heads, bones and skins, then lightly sauté a little celery with some onion and herbs from the garden. I'd strain the liquid and reduce the delicious stock, then would add cubed potato, shredded kippers and peas. A swirl of cream and a little bit of watercress on the top would be the finishing touch. Even my father considered it delicious.'

'It sounds…'

'And I must confess I'm furious that there is now very little to add to my soup - not even an onion to sauté. All I have is pea pods - and they are less than useless.'

'I use pea pods to…'

'It's a travesty how impossible it is to get proper fish. Of course, when I get it, I'm sure to make the stock. Everything has to be used. No waste, remember, Miss Watson.'

'Pea pods…'

'I was desperate last week, Miss Watson. And there it was. Fresh-salted cod at 9d a pound. Of course, I've never before used it. Why would I? I've never used any kind of salted fish, as it really is a substandard product. Because of that, nobody told me it would need soaking for two days and that I should really have asked the fishmonger to soak it beforehand. I bought it, on Tuesday I think it was, and fully expected to eat it that night. I was so disappointed. So very disappointed. As was Mr Armstrong. Inevitably. I can't tell you his disappointment as we made do with barley and leeks that night, and a mutton casserole the night after. And whale! Whale! Did you ever hear of anything more unappetising? Tins of snoek. Tins of whale meat. What on earth…'

'Oh dear,' muttered Penny.

'Oh dear, indeed. Both were flavourless. And that texture! Why did nobody inform me I could have used the fish's soaking water as stock?'

'Can you? Should you?'

Penny's question ignored, Rena went on.

'So, after two days of soaking (and yes, I ensured that I left the fish skin at the top) and a couple of water changes, and wasting a heaped teaspoon of bicarbonate of soda, it was ready. I drained it and cooked it, ready to make soup! Leftover mashed carrots and leftover barley. I drained the fish and rinsed it more than once. I assumed it would be palatable.'

Penny looked at Rena enquiringly.

'It required taming. So poor in comparison with my mackerel soup. So very disappointing.'

'I am sorry, Rena dear.'

'Fish just doesn't seem to cut the mustard nowadays. I tried to make a steamed fish roll, but it was a disaster. I attempted fish in savoury custard, and baked it with turnips and marigold petals from the garden. Obviously, I had to bake that day to ensure I didn't waste the fuel used for the oven. So I used my egg and sugar for a small cake. But no, I can't say I was impressed.'

'Oh dear,' Penny sighed.

'Of course, I'm very conscious of waste and would never leave anything on my plate, but, no. Not pleasant. Do you know what I've found?'

'What's that?' asked Penny.

'That the only palatable way of eating dried or tinned or salted fish - snook, snoek, whale, or whatever - is fried with dripping, chutney, a little gravy powder and a little curry powder. Curried cod. It was the only thing that covered up the revolting taste.'

Penny Watson got up from her friend's kitchen table and smoothed down her hair, then did the same to her skirt.

'Well, Rena, I really must be…

'It's such a terrible situation when you're so short of

supplies. Specially when you're used to so much better. I was reduced to mashing swede with oatmeal and mixing it with the salted cod. They were sausages, of a kind. You know that oatmeal is cheaper at the moment, because of the government subsidies.'

Penny turned to leave but her friend's hand on her arm stopped her.

'Yes, 3d per pound when I bought it last week.'

'I'm sure it was cheaper than that when I bought it the week before. Still, those sausages required a huge amount of rosemary to ensure they didn't suffocate me.'

'Suffocate?' Penny began buttoning her coat.

'Mind you, I should have used carrots. There has been a grand crop this year. The farmers have been working very hard to keep up stocks, and they are so good for one's skin. They keep illness at bay, so I do try to eat as many as I can, don't you?'

Penny sat down again and began unbuttoning her coat.

'I even have them raw on top of cold cooked salad potatoes, with vinegar.'

'Carrot jam is quite nice...'

'Oh no, my dear. Far too sloppy.'

'Oh, I must disagree with you there. I think it is very nice...'

'Well, of course, we can't take your tastebuds as good judges, despite the fact that the Ministry of Food recommends we eat green vegetables and root vegetables every day. I would have done that already. Usually I eat cabbage but it isn't always easy to buy. And nowadays the farmers do better with the carrots and turnips. They keep better you know. And one acquires the greens along with the roots.'

Penny signed and fiddled with the hem of her skirt. A thread was hanging loose and she pulled at it a little.

'My dear. Leave it be. We do not repair our clothing in company, do we? Oh yes, Jackson's Greengrocers gave me a whole basketful of turnip tops. Perfect for the vitamin C and health of one's skin, but Mrs Carlson from next door told me I could soak the white parts in water to root them. One grows a new turnip, and new turnip tops. I made a space in the vegetable patch. You know, the one that used to be the rose bed, and pushed my rooted tops into the earth.'

'So very thrify,' mumbled Penny.

'Of course, marrows also grow so well in this area,

don't they? I make chutney when I can get the sugar and fruit and spices. Other times I can bottle them or dry them. They're so watery, but it's better than nothing, and a bit of a change. Like dried apple rings. They aren't anything like as nice as pies or even the real raw and crispy apples, but they are better than nothing. I do enjoy stuffed marrow and my stuffed cabbage is beautiful. Both are such economical ways to stretch out the meat.'

'I made fish paste with salted cod,' said Penny.

'I'm sure it tasted as horrid as the parsley honey you made.'

'That was a treat. I used all my sugar. It tasted very nice.'

'Nonsense. Nothing like heather honey at all.'

Penny Watson began to shuffle. She was a young woman who lived with two other shop-worker friends. They split their bills but rarely cooked for each other. That meant there would be no supper waiting for her return. The clock on the wall of Rena Armstrong's kitchen said that the time was half past five. She also wanted to be at home for when Peter called. He tended dairy cattle and sometimes brought food gifts to Penny. They'd been courting for more than one year and had both wondered absently if it was perhaps time to marry.

From outside of her thoughts, Penny realised that Rena was still talking.

'...I salted the pile of beans, but they were not successful and I cried for a whole day. Such a terrible waste. Not enough salt, my dear. They went mouldy and mushy.'

'Perhaps you didn't pack...'

'Not enough salt. Nothing to do with how tightly they were packed.'

'Well, Rena, I really must be on my way now,' Penny said as she rose again.

Rena Armstrong finally let her friend go and returned to the kitchen to skim her sheep's head stew.

Penny Watson made her way purposefully back home. All the talk of food did the hungered her, and she returned quickly, without taking the usual share of harvest from the wayside. The lanes were always generous, with their sloes, elderflowers, rowans, nuts, hips and haws. But Penny, despite her hunger, did not stuff anything into her coat pockets.

Instead, she rushed into her kitchen, set her blackberry

leaf and barley water tea to warm, and her lamb breast to roast in the oven, along with the bread she'd left rising that afternoon.

With thoughts of liver and bacon hotpot with dumplings, Penny hoped that the war would end soon.

Bug Out
by Denis Kirkham

I looked over the small rise in the ground at the sight of a full battalion of troops complete with artillery and armoured personnel carriers - maybe three hundred troops all told.

I instantly knew that my small contribution to the war was useless because I was a trooper in allied Special Forces given the task of leading my five man unit. We were to find and destroy what we had been told was nothing more than an axis of evil unit who repaired the communication aerials for their troop commanders. These aerials would direct troops to wherever they were needed.

The first thought I had was that the Intelligence people had got everything so wrong. This was so rare that I forgave them before wondering whatever I could do to complete this mission.

The situation was that I had five troopers, myself and not much else. I wasn't supposed to do much more than take out maybe ten people and to intercept their radio messages for as long as I could safely manage before asking for an air evacuation by Chinook helicopter. Now though I was as good as dead. As soon as I had sent off a message the enemy would have intercepted and immediately tracked them, so all ways up I was screwed.

So I did what I always did and that was to find a spot to hole up, set a sentry and listen to any radio communications being bandied around by the enemy. With the other troopers either eating or sleeping until dark, when we would either do what we could to complete the mission (and be either killed, or injured followed by torture and execution) - or bug out and ask for exfiltration.

We set a stag (sentry) rotation, ate some of the army's worst food ever, and chin wagged to reach some sort of conclusion. The stag had his say even though he was peering out of the depression in the land covered by a camouflage net. We all had a free say in the chin wag, but the final decision was mine, and I would either live or die horribly on the decision I made (as would everyone else).

I agreed to risk a brief and coded message to Camp Bastion even though we knew it would be intercepted - and maybe through the enemy radio detection finder equipment which would home in on us in minutes. The message would be brief, a sit rep (situation report) including position, what we may be able to achieve and whether we could evade capture.

We then settled down and rested as much as we could until nightfall when we would do what was required of us by the Controllers - or what we had discussed and I had decided.

The message was sent in seconds but even so we worryingly saw the enemy sentries look all around them to see if they could see anything. Then some of their troops mounted up in troop carriers and began to circle their camp in ever increasing circles. This meant we had minutes to either dig in some more and pray we wouldn't be found, or begin an immediate retreat asking for air support.

What a decision.

I took the decision to dig in, hide our position and just hope we wouldn't be found. We were banking on the enemy not being bothered to do that much in the heat and almost flat terrain, and we were right, thankfully. They drove around for half an hour then made their way back to their camp. We breathed again and smiled at each other. We knew we had escaped death by a whisker so had a drink. It wasn't a pint in a pub but cold tea was more than enough.

The Controllers radioed in using a microwave system. The message was sent so fast and so coded that even if discovered it would mean nothing without our decoder. They asked us, or more accurately told us, to sit tight, watch and report and only begin aggression if there was no other course of action. We smiled at that one, but they had allocated us a helicopter armed and ready to respond to us within minutes. We felt happier in some ways, but in other ways left out to dry. We were on our own and seconds from death, but also minutes from escape. We set up an OP (observation position), dug in, made our positions as camouflaged as possible and began a system of watches, stag (sentry), and waited until sun down.

If we thought our position was risky as it was, the day afterward things ramped up a whole lot more.

There's not much a soldier despises more than another soldier who doesn't 'buy into' the mission, and now Corporal Jones had raised the bar way above any incompetence he had reached before (and saying that, I was aware that he was a level one spot on numpty).

What did he do? He only broadcast our position to the enemy by radioing our next sit rep without coding. He did this because he thought that none of the enemy would know English.

When I educated him by holding him in a headlock and threatening him with death (which at that time I really meant), I asked him when he was on holiday to Dubai how many Middle Eastern people spoke perfect English. Once he thought for two nano seconds (which isn't long) he mumbled some kind of apology to the patrol. That was nice but it didn't get us out of our predicament that once the enemy had intercepted our transmission we would no doubt be under threat from both ground and air forces - and as good as dead.

I considered killing Jones but the blood and guts would alert the birds that always flew around groups in the desert and give us away. Even so, it took the other troopers to drag me off his windpipe.

Soldering is a deadly game. It was really deadly when you are behind enemy lines - as we were. I had marked his card and he knew it.

We (or I) had to decide what to do. Bug out and hopefully reach a rv (rendezvous) point for a heli lift? Or march and die?

It was not much of a choice, I guess, so as a group we had to look at the maps we had and the most recent radio messages. This was to try and work out an escape route, but we soon discovered there wasn't one.

So, we decided to raid the enemy base and inflict as much damage as we could manage before the dash back to our rv point. Then heli support back to somewhere I would rip Jones's head off tendon by tendon.

At least I had something to dream about, but Jones couldn't say anything so he got the bag job. The bag job is the person who sits behind the person having a number two into a plastic bag so that we can leave any spot without anyone knowing we were ever there. A number two would be a dead giveaway. So Jones had the job of bag holding while we all dropped our kecks and did one as often as we could. And Jones had the job of carrying it all in his bergen - not forgetting our urine.

We all had what could be loosely termed 'loose' bowels but Jones manfully did his job. We all laughed at the prospect of his nose being peeled away by the fumes, knowing he would have to manage his own bagging because none of us would help him and you had to be a dab hand with your aim otherwise your digits got a bit involved. It was all the more difficult when we repeatedly called him just when concentration was needed to be at a maximum.

He deserved it. He really did. So we laid into him.

He got the message.

The enemy were more active than they had been an hour ago but didn't seem overly so and certainly didn't appear to be looking for anyone. So we packed our kit, buried what we didn't need if we were to bug out, and made sure the camouflage net was laid over us without any neat edges.

We waited with stag every ninety compass points and no talking other than in a genuine whisper. Noise travels far in the desert, so we whispered like washerwomen in a church.

Nothing happened to alert us that we might have been compromised, so we stayed were we were until nightfall. That was when we decided to see how close to the enemy we could get and if it was possible to do some damage before bugging out.

We all crept along on our belt buckles. That is an army term for crawling lower than a flat rattle snake. We were very slowly getting closer to the enemy camp when we heard the noise of troops. They were being as unprofessional as only Taliban could be when they felt safe and when they had some alcohol. They couldn't have that back at their base. Anyway, they were as drunk as lords and as noisy as an Irish pub on St Patrick's night.

We got as close to the boundary of their camp as we could without actually being seen ourselves. We may not have been visible, but could see three fuel bowsers, four 10 ton troop carrying trucks, four armoured personnel carriers and two four wheel drive trucks with mounted machine guns.

Let's be honest - the fuel bowsers were our top priority along with the aerials. If we could knock out both the bowsers and the radio shack we could just about consider an audacious escape bug out.

They had made a very poor tactical move by placing all the vehicles around the fuel bowsers. This may have been to make refuelling easier (who knows?). But we realised that one big bang could wipe out most of them.

We made maps on our digestible paper pads and then retraced our steps back to our observation point ready to plan and rest, all except Jones who had the job of bag holder as often as we could manage our bowels to move even a touch. He knew it was bullying and we knew it too, but he was screwed and we loved it.

We decided to try to knock out the bowsers using only the explosives we had in our bergens. We didn't have much, but placed strategically, we could totally destroy one and rupture the other two. This would hopefully create one massive bish bash bosh of burning fuel. This would take two of us and the other three would stag us, then after the bonfire started we would knock out the aerials they used for comms using a grenade launcher on one of our SA80 standard issue rifles.

We were confident we could manage the job, but we would then have to bug out faster than a Jaguar on speed. Either that or we could audaciously stay put and dug in, with no sign whatsoever. Unless someone stood on the camo netting which we would place over our OP and then sprinkle with sand and stones. That would render us as close to invisible as we could be.

We talked it over and decided the last place the enemy would look would be right under their noses, so we would stay put and save both energy and rounds. It was audacious enough to work, and we knew we could hit them for six in a firefight, so it was decided stay put.

We dug our OP a bit deeper and worked hard on the camouflage side of things, then rested up because we were to attack that night just before dawn. If we attacked before then they would still have stags who would be awake. Most Taliban stags in Afghan' seemed to see sleep as more important than watching. Their belief in 'Inshalla' which means 'if it is the will of God' meant they didn't need to watch because what happened was out of their control anyway.

But round about five am was known as the time that people were at their lowest ebb. It was accepted in hospitals that four to five am was the time when people could be expected to die. That's how it was and we decided to use it to our advantage and make some Taliban proof of that.

At 0400 we prep'd our kit, with full magazines, grenades fixed to our rifles, night sight goggles on, plan fixed in our heads and eyes and ears switched on. We were high on adrenalin and slowly belt buckled to the fence.

We could see their stags well asleep. There was no-one awake and we could hear lots of snoring, so we knew we could do it. We shook each others hands. We even included Jones's hand, even knowing where it had been.

We went for it. Here goes. It really was do or die. We were hoping that the death would be quick and not via torture in some flea pit with sweaty Taliban laughing as we slowly and painfully expired.

We cut the wire as low as possible and crept under the fence, one soldier to be left behind to cut a larger hole in the fence for our bug out, and to watch the enemy stag troops for any sign of life.

The other four of us split into two pairs. One pair went for their positions to lob some grenades into the radio shack, while me and Jones went for the fuel bowsers with our plastic explosive with three minute fuses. They were fast fuses and we knew we wouldn't be able to waste time getting to the hole in the fence. We'd cut the hole on the opposite side of the fence to our OP so the enemy would search for us in the wrong area.

Jones and I crept to the bowsers with our eyes and ears on maximum, and with night-sight goggles giving us a green coloured picture. Once we got switched on we normalised it, and creeping slowly forward we fixed ourselves right under the first bowser. Jones placed the explosive right onto the weakest place on the bowser which was on the welds at its rear, facing the other two bowsers. We were hoping the flames would blast across the gap and rupture to other two bowsers.

Jones was superb at his speciality - which was explosives - and quickly set the device. We leopard-crawled out, signalling to the other two that they had less than three minutes to wait until the fireworks began. As soon as we were all together at the fence they launched the grenades into the radio shack. This was followed less than a minute later with an almighty whoosh and bang of fuel tanks rupturing and fuel forced out and firing into the most beautiful sight. We thought it would be, anyway.

The enemy troops were just pitiful, running around with their kit all over the place. Some were dressed and some not. Some were with rifles but most without. There was no-one in charge and we just laughed and bugged out to our OP and dug in watching the light show from front row seats.

True to expectation, the Taliban just ran around with their hands waving around doing nothing. The stags were stood still staring into space trying to find something to lock onto. They must have found some shadow somewhere and they fired round after round into the night as far away from us as you could possibly be. We smiled but remained eyes on, two with night sight goggles, and two without. Just watching and waiting as one of them must surely know what to do.

But it was like a circus, with everything happening

inside the camp and nothing anywhere else. The fires slowly diminished and the night became dark again, but one thing we did notice was no-one in their camp was using night sight goggles - so we had an advantage from the off.

They just stood wondering what to do next. Not one of them had been shot in a fire fight, and no-one had been injured as far as we could see, so we assumed that they had no idea how it had all happened. This was much to our advantage. Then someone must have twigged to the fact that their radio shack had been compromised by some action or other, and then some of them climbed to their to stag points and looked around the desert to see if there were any sign of troops or aircraft.

It was then that we realised they thought it was an airborne attack, and that until they found the gap in the wire we would remain distanced from the attack. We'd stitched up the gap as good as time had allowed.

The day dawned and the sight we had was of just about as much total destruction as there could be. There were no fuel bowsers so no fuel, no radio shack so no radio comms, and nobody seemingly knowing what to do. That was until a young officer gathered the troops and pointed to the destroyed radio shack and fuel bowsers. We could see him asking troops to check the fuel situation in the vehicles they had. Unfortunately for them they didn't appear to have much, and certainly not enough to travel back to the supply road.

He visibly wobbled - no fuel, no comms, stuck in the middle of nowhere with slack troops and no camp infrastructure. What would be next for them? It would certainly not be a Beau Geste yomp out of the desert, so they arranged themselves in rows, faced east and began to pray.

They needed it, but so did we. We couldn't bug out with them staying where they were. We needed them to move out and let us bug out then call in a helicopter for evacuation. We hadn't thought about what they would do - or rather I hadn't - and we were going nowhere slowly. But at least we had Jones to do the bag duties, seeing how no-one had come to relieve him.

Sorry Jones.

Our team...

'Bag man' Jones, our explosive specialist, had been a member of the Paras and applied for selection to Special Forces when he was nineteen. He passed first time. This railed some members who thought he was immature - and to an extent they were right - but to give him his due he had worked hard and here he was a year out from selection, playing a full and active part in our warfare. He was good, very good, and would only get better. Even now he's being considered for promotion.

Deano, the Welsh warrior, applied for selection from the Welsh Guards which surprised us because he wasn't even Welsh per se. His mother was though, and he chose to take that side of his family line and become Welsh using the explanation that a dog born in a stable isn't a horse.

This was true, but we gave him so much stick. If they had been pound coins he would have been very rich.

He was annoyingly good at everything but in his skill as a medic specialist he was fantastic. If my life should be hanging by a thread I would ask for him. He was twenty nine, had been with us for four years, and his skill set had become top drawer. He was a good man.

Cope was a communication specialist and sniper trained young gun, a brilliant shot, and very good comms. He could repair, rebuild and sort out anything that was asked of him. He came to us from the Rifles, which was not the normal pathway, but he made the grade and he was here with us aged thirty one. He was the only one of us married. Personally I didn't think it a good idea to be married, but he had a skill where he could zone out for months on end, never wavering from his task. Cope was a good trooper.

Then there's me, Kirky, the navigation specialist and troop leader. I came from the usual route of Two Para, selection at twenty two, troop leader at twenty six and here I am at thirty.

I love the special forces. I love the danger and the informality of the troop but I have always invested 100% and am known as a tough but fair boss. Having said that, I have never suffered fools at all. One avoidable gaff, and as far as you were concerned you were no longer on my radar.

Ralph the mechanics specialist was the oldest among us at thirty nine, but he was as fit and strong as anyone I've met in the troop, He was a man mountain. Annoy him and you would be launched from a window and wouldn't get home before your next birthday. I liked him and would walk over hot coals for him. Even though I was Troop Commander I always gave him respect. He deserved it. He was a top man.

There we were, five specialists and five 100% courageous troopers who never turned away from a task and always fought for each other.

'Never Leave Anyone Behind' was our unofficial motto. The true motto was something in Latin, but seeing now nobody spoke Latin, ours would do just fine.

We had a meeting and gathered our thoughts. Everyone had an equal say and I listened to all the comments. The decision was made to dig in, cammo up, keep silent and watch, ready with considerable firepower and courage. We would be ready to die for one another and not one of us would surrender, or desert our position, unless captured. The sides were ready, the rules disbanded and nerves just enough on edge to ready our reflexes.

Bring it on.

The morning found the Taliban almost working as a team - some digging graves, some erecting a clean new tent for a crude field hospital, and the officer working his socks off to do the best he could. Collectively we admired that but we also knew that he was to be Copes' target as sniper. One shot, with night sight, silencer and muzzle suppressor fitted and it would be 'Goodbye Vienna'.

That night, as soon as it became dark and the Taliban began drinking alcohol (and who could blame them) the officer left his shack for a fag when the other men, apart from their stags, were drunk and sleeping. One silent shot fired at 4800kph flew straight into his head. It was a clean entry but messy exit taking half his face with it.

He was dead as soon it hit. At least it was painless. The stags knew nothing about it until dawn and the first hungover Taliban found his leader dead. It looked like suicide but they couldn't find a weapon. They then freaked out big time and we 'firmed up' ready for a firefight. But all they did was wail and face east.

We looked around with binoculars and telescopic sights, but saw no danger other than hunger. We told ourselves that at this rate we would win by default. We brewed some coffee and chomped some high energy bars while they just ran around doing nothing. We were considering an emergency helicopter evacuation when we saw with horror a line of vehicles coming towards us with reinforcement Taliban.

It was an enemy armoured personnel carrier stick of around six vehicles with another six half ton lorries behind, no doubt full of troops, the whole stick no doubt responding to a lack of comms contact.

We were screwed this time, I thought. There were five of us and around fifty of the enemy. With our skills, that was a winnable fight, we decided, laughing. Knowing the truth, we would be cannon fodder, and unless we bugged out we would be toast.

The enemy reached the camp at dusk and appeared to concentrate on repairing the comms and treating their buddies, before setting stags and looking round the camp wire and finding our escape spot cut into it. They did what we thought they would do and began a tentative search on the opposite side of the camp to our OP. That went on until nightfall and gave us time to have a chin wag and come to the conclusion there was no future in our being where we were.

So we prepared to bug out.

We cleared our camp to sterile cleanliness, and collected every ounce of evidence that said we had been there. Thanks to Jones there was no poo as it was all in bags in our bergens. It was the same with pee and food containers. There were no labels to be taken off food cans as we had removed them at camp before deploying. We left no sign whatsoever, even sprinkling some goats' poo we had found on our deployment after the heli ride in. When discovered, the depression would be thought of as a goat herder's camp.

We not only looked damned cool but we had brains as well. Not the Welsh beer drunk by Jones, but grey matter matched by ferocious and extreme violence when needed.

We were Special Forces and not just that, but British Special Forces. We knew we were better than any other Special Forces and that made us so confident it was ludicrous to even contemplate our failure.

When it was dark and we figured that the new troops would be asleep after a long desert journey, we bugged out. We made progress due east to an area of mixed ground, some hills, some wadis and some clearings with 360 degree sight. We hoped that would allow a helicopter evacuation back to civilisation and to beers all round. Except Jones who only drank Brains beer. We admired the dedication he showed to his drink but we had bought every can to be found and dug a hole for them all. It was a bumper wheeze and we even had a treasure map for him to follow, but it started in Cardiff so we knew he couldn't find it unless he carried out a forfeit. He had to empty all our poo and wee bags into the camp latrine. Nothing to it for a red dragon.

We laughed at the prospect even though we were some hundred kms inside enemy lines with nothing except ourselves and our weapons, but we would do it just for Jones' sake.

We had however one very serious problem. We were running very short of water and only had a couple of days before we would need some more. We might have been tough soldiers but were still only human, and water was crucial. Three days without it and we would be dead. That was a simple fact. No heroics would save you.

During the 17th and 18th centuries it was common practice for shipwrecked sailors in ships' lifeboats to draw lots. The loser got killed and his blood would be drunk and flesh eaten to satisfy both hunger and thirst of the rest of the crew.

I couldn't see any of my unit agreeing to this, so I filed it under 'maybe' and as we talked this through we decided that if we saw evidence of goats we would take one and use it to give us something to drink and eat. It sounds barbaric, but so is dying of thirst in the desert.

We moved east during the first night before setting up a camp with stags every two hours, with orders to obviously awake everyone if people were seen, or if animals we could use came along. But sleeping during the day in a desert isn't easy. It is hot and sweaty. The night time bugging is the opposite. Cold and tiring.

We needed rest, food and water. It wasn't even a maybe. Sometime after twelve midday the stag woke us up asking us to firm up because he had seen evidence of movement a distance away and wanted other opinions of it. We all trained our eyes and binos on the dust trace and saw the incredible sight of a Fordson Major tractor coming towards us with a trailer carrying animals and what looked like barrels.

We wet our lips at this sight. It was so bizarre I thought it was a mirage until we all confirmed it was a tractor. It took three nano seconds to decide to intercept and pilfer the trailer before deciding what to do with the driver. We didn't want to kill him unless he made himself compromised by his actions. What would be would be.

We estimated that the tractor must be around four hundred metres away and was travelling along at a speed that would make it ready to intercept in a couple of minutes. A 'stand up' procedure would suffice. That meant we would all stand up in front of the tractor with only one man checking our rear. We hoped the driver wouldn't try to be a hero and would stop when he saw four guns held by four desperados in a mix of soldiers' clothing and Arab shemaques, wearing Ray Ban sunglasses.

We quickly spread out along the route the tractor seemed to be travelling - which was a straight line due west. He was following the sun for his western bearing and as we were travelling east we would have the elements of not only surprise, but of the sun as our backdrop. We slowly moved across the desert on our belt buckles, fanning out to form a semi-circle around him, and we waited until my signal before slowly but confidently raising up to confront him.

The driver was bumbling along, heaven knows where to or from, but just bumbling along singing the latest Arab hit song and chewing some tobacco, when four men slowly stood up in front of him, rifles pointing at him, and sunglasses giving an air of menace. He nearly jumped off the tractor in shock, saying some swear words in Pashtun but instead he thought of speeding up and gunning it - until his Mr Sensible head took over. He stopped the tractor and jumped down saying 'Inshalla' (if it is Gods will) and knelt down on his knees ready for the single head shot that would finish him off before Paradise took over.

He wasn't so lucky. We restrained him with plastic cable ties and began a search of his load. Bingo. Water, bread, goats' meat and some mutton. It was still really fresh as it was alive so he hadn't come to far from a town or village. The water was fresh as well, but we filtered it through personal filters before drinking it, then we ate some meat and bread and offered him some as well as the goats. But he just kept saying 'Inshalla' and kneeling down in front of us all.

Ah well, just because his vocabulary was limited we still ate, and he didn't.

Deano spoke some Arabic and found out there was a town 10 kms west and one 14kms east. We decided to use the tractor for our travels and to keep the driver with us because we hadn't the heart to leave him wandering in the desert in his sandals. We decided that as it was almost nightfall we would move to the nearest shelter we could find for the rest of day. We would be keeping stag rotation at two hours.

We had liberated the goats and we had travelled no more than two klicks east when we spotted a small wadi. It was no more than a few trees and some rocks but that was plenty for us to cam up against and be almost undetectable.

Then we saw it about a mile away. A huge dark sandstorm. We knew we had only a few seconds to prepare for it. Just enough time to cover our faces with our shemaques and to lie down under the trailer until it passed. We were covered head to toe in fine sand. It got everywhere inside our clothes, our noses and ears.

But after the fast clear brush off we found to our horror that the driver had gone and there was no sign of Jonno. We wondered if he had found the driver running away and gone after him but we found Jonno's weapon where he left it under a rug on the trailer. He wouldn't have gone anywhere without his weapon. This was the top rule of Special Forces - to always take your weapon.

So Jonno had been taken hostage by the driver, but where to? It left us missing an operator. Not only that, but he always carried his explosives kit with him. Not explosives as such but fuses and detonators which were kept separate from the explosives themselves.

But where were they? There seemed nothing but desert all around, but there must have been something or somewhere for him to hide away from our eyes. We waited, which was the usual response to kidnappings in a desert. After all what else was there to do, realistically? They must show themselves soon so we set 360 degree stags. If he as much as twitched we would see him. After an hour we began to talk to each other trying to bounce ideas between us. We discussed the things they wouldn't be able to do, leading us to at least one possible and one probable idea, but they were more desperate than inspired. We even checked under the trailer on the off chance they were underneath it. This was truly desperate, but so were we.

We reckoned the reason we couldn't see them was because the Arab must have been one of the enemy's own Special Forces. Things could and would become that much more difficult, a bit like playing chess with sixteen pieces each of the same value. Nobody would have any advantage over the other so it was down to mistakes.

Who made the first mistake would lose.

We decided that we had to continue going east. It was tough, but why should we all lose because one of us was kidnapped. He would realise that and agree with it, so we dug in for the day and began that night using the tractor.

We made good speed and kept a constant watch for our pal but we saw nothing and heard nothing. We had to move on and put it behind us.

After six hours we were sixty miles from our last OP, and as the sun would come up soon we stopped and dug in, ate and drank. Our water again was running out and we only used the minimum amount for our work. It was a dividing line between being topped up enough to be effective soldiers and being topped up not enough so becoming liabilities.

Two hours into our rest and the earth shook, bullets flew all around us, the screams and whoops disoriented us as we were attacked by enemy militia. They were everywhere, or so it seemed. One of the stag troops asked for covering fire as he had seen an opening into the enemy position. We put down maximum fire to clear a path for him to run down. We had to be careful to aim around him or we could shoot him ourselves, blue on blue.

We'd practised this time and time again back in Hereford but it's not quite the same in action. We watched him swerve from side to side after giving us an almost imperceptible sign. It worked because we were the best in the business. The SAS: the illustrious fighting force of the United Kingdom.

The voice came back to us that there were at least fifty enemies surrounding us in an arc with mortars being set up as he spoke. They wore the black berets of the Kings Fusiliers.

We knew we would probably all die here in the desert sand where we would be denied any help from our government because we were acting without official support.

We felt like turkeys in November.

We knew that we would die, just not exactly when or exactly how. Would it be the painless round to the head or heart or the torture of sadistic nutters who would dismantle our bodies extremity by extremity. We had been told, unofficially of course, that if captured we could have body parts removed then would be left waiting while the stumps healed before having something else removed by the most painful method. We had heard the horror stories of forearms being torn from the elbows, and feet being twisted round and round until they were only held on by sinew. It was beyond comprehension that we would have to watch dogs eat our body parts.

We were in it deep, and we saw no way out. Death was coming fast one way or the other and we had nothing to fight back with other than SA80 rifles with limited rounds, small arms in the shape of Browning 5mm pistols and a handful of grenades.

I remembered the song 'Always Look on the Bright Side of Life' and smiled to myself. There was no bright side here, and in a few short minutes there would likely be no life either. Like the others, I had decided that if there was a realistic chance of being taken prisoner we would save the last bullet for ourselves or would booby trap our body by hooking the pin of a grenade into our body armour chest plate. By just a small movement of our body we would release the pin from its secure tenure and detonate the grenade five seconds afterwards.

With luck our body armour would shatter and make shards of shrapnel seriously giving one of the Kings Fusiliers a shock he wasn't expecting when he blasted into the air in tatters. At the very least we would lie on the pin of a grenade, dead.

In case a round had torn into our body, killing or seriously injuring before we could detonate our grenade, there would be an enemy who'd be given the job of checking us over for maps etc. He would earn himself a war wound about two foot long by six inches wide wearing his best beret as it flew into the earth's orbit.

We were ready and primed. We were literally revved up, high on adrenalin and with fingers twitching the trigger. We were ready to spoil someone's day by giving them a very short but very painful realisation of who the SAS really were - the best in the business of extreme violence. Then we heard above the racket of warfare the almost inaudible but unmistakeable sound of the Apache attack helicopter, and there was clearly more than one. Then we saw the fire flame of a round being released from its barrel and the thud and almost instantaneous boom of the explosion. This scattered the enemy from the immediate theatre of war.

Some might say it would have been more humane to have them in one piece but we weren't bothered that they would have been converted into molecules.

The pilots and gunners using the best night sights in the world were a sight to see. Maybe the sight would even be better if we were where they were, but still front stall seats to this kind of fire fight were good enough for us.

Slowly we saw the enemy dematerialise into body parts. Some tried running towards us, but they were easy meat for us and were doing us a favour by allowing us to join in the fun. Those who tried to run away from us were mincemeat for the Apache back up helicopters who professionally destroyed their day.

Within minutes the whole battle plan had changed from self-detonation to loud cheers and whoops, though we were still watchful for any stray enemy who played dead just to fire that one round at 4800 km an hour into your hairstyle.

We weren't that bothered, to be honest, as lines with tethers on them were dropped from each heli and we each latched onto one. It was one man per heli so that if one was compromised we wouldn't lose the whole unit. We were lifted up from hell on earth into hell in the sky slowly turning so we didn't spin round too much. During training the Apache pilots deliberately made us spin round so fast we could have blacked out. This was so we would be able to withstand the motion, or at least believe in the pilot's skill.

But for some unfortunate who would have had too much beer the night before, the motion of spinning wasn't the only motion he felt. But what the hell. We were rescued from certain death, so some spinning was the penance we would merrily bear.

As we were travelling fast away from the action one of the side doors of one of the helicopters opened and there he was. It was Jonno. How on earth? One minute he was a prisoner and the next the hero being awarded the Military Cross for his soldiering and courage as a top soldier and one whose citation would be pinned up on the notice board in the regimental bar back in Hereford.

His story was so incredulous it wasn't instantly believable. He'd been sheltering from the sandstorm, as we all were, when he felt the unmistakeable metal of a gun barrel pressing slowly onto his neck. Scenarios played in his mind instantly - shout a warning which wouldn't be heard, fight back and die. But putting his hands up would give him the chance to plan some sort of reaction to his predicament. So it was hands up.

The mystery Arab was one of the Black Fusiliers Commando Troop - the elite. To put this into some seniority, most of these, or at least their training staff were trained themselves, with the USA SEALS, the French Foreign Legion's Second Foreign Parachute Regiment, the Deuxieme Rep and shamefully our own SAS - while they seemed our friends and not our foes. You could tell those trained by the SEALS because they spoke with the kind of accent used for children's cartoons. Those trained by the Legion Entrangere spoke in pidgin French like some singer at the Eurovision song contest trying to sing in French. Those trained by us spoke a midland accent. It was damned good fun teaching someone to fight using a Jasper Carrott accent. This one said 'OK buddy, it's time to hike. You've got ten seconds to decide whether I'll use this to drill into your brain. It's a yes or a no question. Stay low or I blow your head off. You decide,' just like Clint Eastwood in the Dirty Harry movies. He was American-trained which meant he would be good, very good - but sometimes calling his own bluff. He stood a chance of outwitting his enemy but he would be given one chance to either use it well or blow it. He laughed when he thought of Clint Eastwood and imagining it being something he might have said.

    The Arab had managed to slowly work himself backwards from his position into a slight depression fifty metres back. Fifty metres in a sandstorm was like earth and moon. He then dug out extra depth to the depression then rolled Jonno into the depression first before arranging him into a position of facing upwards and doing the same himself. Then he reached inside his clothing and brought out two large diameter drinking straws with camouflage by grass fronds, then wrapped Jonno up good and proper with more cable ties so he couldn't move at all. If he had, the straw would be dislodged and that would be very bad for Jonno because the Arab began pulling sand over them until they were completely hidden. The sand storm did the rest by arranging the surface sand exactly the same as the next patch of sand.

    It was a brilliant special forces tactic, and one he hadn't heard of before except in water, but to use it in a desert and to succeed using it meant many hours of training and many failures until it was perfected. Using it meant complete compliance from the prisoner and therefore the perfect prisoner guard was the prisoner themself.

    When the sand storm passed over and Jonno could think about escape, he was still well and truly trussed up and he remained like that all that day and night covered in sand and held prisoner by the breathing straw. He didn't see the Arab slowly levering himself up and breathing some sand away - just enough to allow him to watch the Special Forces looking around, probing and scanning the area with binoculars. As night fell he used night vision and thermal imagining cameras trying to find any heat responses that would signify either an animal or a person. But hidden under sand there were no signs of heat returned. As far as the Special Forces were concerned, they had disappeared. How or when was a mystery - a very scary mystery - because it signalled the skill of another Special Forces operative.

His own Special Forces had left as there was no other action they could take. The longer they stayed put with a very capable enemy somewhere in the area, the more they became sitting ducks. However, the Arab had not only seen them leave but had put together a radio transmitter he had hidden within a body cavity - just as some prisoners are known to do. He had sent out a signal that relayed his position and the fact he was alive and that the enemy had fallen for the ruse of a lone man on a tractor. As he did this he smiled to himself and thanked God for his care over him. 'Inshalla,' he said over and over again.

Once they were alone, the Arab brushed the sand from around Jonno and released most of his cable ties so that he could stand, but not much else. He could also relieve himself which he desperately needed. This wasn't just to relieve his body, but to leave a scent trail should his own forces come back with dogs to try to trace him. At least they would know he was alive after they had left. The Arab used the transmitter as GPS - a global positioning system receiver that would pinpoint any waymark plotted into it with an accuracy of one metre. The waymark he sought was for a supply dump where he would find small arms, food, water and a more powerful radio which he could use to ask for a helicopter to exfiltrate himself with a prisoner.

Jonno waited and watched the Arab closely - he was so intensely employed in his work radioing his position and his status that he didn't see Jonno slowly almost imperceptibly moving closer and closer. He had no clear cut plan, just a need to get as physically close to him as he could, while waiting for the one opportunity to turn the table and become the dominant one. His training wass geared up to becoming number one if in a capture situation. The one thing impressed into their mentality was to be the dominant one, even if you don't appear to be. To be one of the best, either as a team or as a single person. He saw the radio transmitter and couldn't believe his luck when he recognised it as a type used by Special Forces worldwide with the internal workings altered to their own requirements.

Bingo! If he could get his hands on it he would be in with a chance but that would require him to release his hands from the bindings. Without this he couldn't get any closer to freedom than he was now.

His guard was so intent on his own jobs that it was as if he had forgotten about Jonno who moved closer and closer to him with a position on the ground where he would be able to slightly raise his hips and deliver a blow from a karate style kick. That would wind him to say the least.

His kick came with a level of ferociousness which enabled that his capturer was not only winded, but completely immobilised. Jonno did this by putting him in a headlock with his feet while grabbing the radio and using one of its edges to cut through the cable ties on his hands, and to allow him to tie the Arab who'd left some cable ties out in the open.

Now the tables were turned, and knowing the Arab had radioed their position and requested a heli for exfiltration, he hadn't much time. Every operator learned enough Arabic to give them a fighting chance if it was needed and he knew he had given their position as some two kms away. Why? He didn't know. Maybe it was a fuel dump in case the heli needed a refuelling, but he knew that this meant the enemy heli wouldn't be able to return to their base without refuelling. He slightly changed the tuning of the transmitter. Every operator had two skills. Jonno's primary skill was explosives but he also had been taught much about radios and comms. He had managed to tap out his position by Morse code as they were outside the operating range for speech. He requested an exfiltrate, gave the position of an enemy fuel dump, and gave the route his own unit had set off on.

What the base radio tech's heard was nothing short of a miracle because they had all been presumed either dead, missing in action or prisoners. The army machine began to turn and a squadron of Apache attack helicopters were readied for immediate deployment with maximum firepower and crews experienced enough to be left to their own devices, to an extent.

The Apaches deployed and began the flight to rescue Jonno and to capture the Arab for interrogation. With joy, Jonno heard the distinctive whine of an Apache's engines and not one, but an entire squadron. Once he had been lifted off the ground and was able to communicate properly with his officers he found the pilots taking animatedly. They had found a source of some sort of action on their land radar and they agreed to go and have a look. After all, it would make their day perfect if they could attack the enemy before breakfast.

The pilots saw a half circle of militia marching towards a band of maybe four or five soldiers who were on their exfil route of their own Special Forces unit. It was with absolute pleasure and after identification by radio that they weighed in and joined the party. They left no-one who wasn't either dead, injured or prisoner and the whole unit knew they had taken a lead part in a mission that would live for eternity in the annals of the Special Air Service.

Hero? Not from where I'm standing!
by Delia Southern

They're calling me a hero.
It's very annoying and it's embarrassing because it's not true.
Who are they? Mainly the newspapers,
But even my friends and family are looking sideways at me,
Not sure whether to be cross because I never said anything,
Or proud because people are saying
that I have done something good.

But I know that, in the same position,
anyone else would have done the same.
I didn't choose - there was no option.
If you see that something needs to be done, you just do it.
You can't do anything else. So what's heroic about that?
Was I scared? Of course I was. I'm not a fool.
But you just don't think about that; you get on with it.

Not because of love for your fellow man,
or any of the silly things they are saying.
But because the job needs doing. Now, this minute.
So I'm annoyed and embarrassed;
I wish they would leave me alone.

A Soldier's Prayer
by Sally James

I was told that the soldiers in WW1 were given two books - The Rubaiyyat of Omar Khayaam and the Bible. I attempted to get into the head of a soldier going into battle. I read a few verses of the Rubaiyyat which put me in the mood to write this poem.

You told me that the sun spills early gold
To herald in a new day dawning
I see only the mist of battle hovering
Like a damp shroud grey with mourning.

So I rise and hold my bayonet to the sky
My heart you say must fill each precious day
Listen hear my startled battle cry
And together may your fingers pray.

Is this to be the rarest day for me?
Is this not the day that you my Lord I see?
Now you say there is no single taker
Fight your war then meet your maker.

I long may sigh that I may never repossess
That bowl of crystal pure red wine
This makes me feel so truly dispossessed
So I stand oblivious on this first and final line.

Here where every branch is scorched by heat of gun
Where every breeze ne'er feels the morning sun
Where every bough bends with the stench of fear
I pray that in my battle storm, that you my Lord can hear.

The most glorious morning now I see
A new beginning my victory
And now from every sallow face on corpse of man
I remember that it was from sacred dust our bone began.

I should feel guilt but you have freed me from my sin
My Lord I cry, I see your house, I enter in
As blast and shot shudder around my head
My cries lie dormant with my comrades, wounded, dead.

And so life passes, I drink on, and fill my empty cup once more
For I am safe, God did not knock upon my door
I sip my wine and savour this cup bittersweet
I march on and on, my life you tell me, not yet complete.

I rest in rose's shade though winds
Have burst the blossom of the few
Now here I lie amongst the petals and as they fall
And in my sleep I dream of you.

The draught of scorched wind burns my face
I cannot rest and dream within this sweetest place
Forward marching as one hundred shots ring clear
Oh, my Lord at last I see your face, I feel you near.

For as the sun shines so the moon must sail her way
My night can be no darker than my day
My Lord is with me, he holds my hand
He leads me to another world, a Promised Land.

A Pantoum About the Somme July 1ˢᵗ 1916
by Sally James

I watched a film about the Somme.
Young men going to their death.
Sixty thousand casualties in two hours.
Their battle lost as it began.

Young men going to their death.
Innocence mixed with sad regret.
Their battle lost as it began.
A lesson we must not forget.

Innocence mixed with sad regret.
How many times have we to learn?
A lesson we must not forget.
There is no sense in bloody wars.

How many times have we to learn?
How much carnage must we endure?
There is no sense in bloody wars.
It makes children cry and widows weep.

How much carnage must we endure?
I watched a film about the Somme.
It makes children cry and widows weep.
Sixty thousand casualties in first two hours.

Death Day
by Denis Kirkham

A sweet and bewildered face.

The day was the same as yesterday and the yesterday of that day. It was hot. Too hot and dry. Energy-sapping, dehydrating and what we called a 'death day'. The brain cannot absorb information in that heat. It feels like you have a lazy brain, like being drunk.

You look but cannot see and you listen, but you don't hear. The click of a rifle that is having the safety taken off. The small depression under your foot of the IED pressure plate. Life changing moments, life or death, legs or stumps, pain and blood, too fast, too late - a death day moment.

The compound or village was about one hundred and fifty yards square, surrounded by a six-foot wall with one entrance. Homes were inside made of dried mud, the huts about six feet high, ten feet long and six-foot-wide, all made of clay and without windows. The smell coming from the huts was of turmeric, cardamom and garlic, and outside there were children playing like all children do. Laughing and running in their barefeet, the boys wearing hats and the girls' hijabs.

The day began as all soldiers' days do. It was time to wake up, scratch, cough, drink coffee and eat another bag of army ration of porridge or dried eggs - none of which tasted anything like their name. More coffee and a fag, and more coughs. Why stop smoking when every day could be your last?

We were all awake and ready by 06:00. Time to do our gear, body armour, belt kit, radios and helmets, and tourniquets placed around our upper thighs to save time if our legs were blown off. Time to leave our camp in the wadi and move up to our next rendezvous point in the village of Ham-In-Lash in Lash-Na-Ghar province at the end of our patrol. Before then we would visit the villages along the way.

Our remit was to meet the locals and do what we could medically for them. We were a unit of six paramedics from the Army Medical Corp and six Royal Marines, and we were to show them love and give medical aid where we could.

As you'd see in all war zones there were plenty of casualties from the instruments of war. There were children with limbs missing due to landmines, sharp edged shell casings and burns from unexploded incendiary bombs that detonated when their pressure plate was detonated. The trouble was IEDs, burns from unexploded incendiary bombs, and shell casings that were razor sharp but made perfect holders for lots of domestic items. We never knew when the wounds of war would come their way - or ours.

The Taliban dressed the same as peaceful people, not unlike the terrorists in the Troubles in Northern Ireland. One Afghani looked like any other Afghani, dish-dash, sandals, hat and a Honda Hero motorcycle. But sometimes they had an AK47 tucked away under their dish-dash, or an IED ready for placing and arming. But we always looked the same, with battle dress and weapons ready but on their safety, and radios with tall aerials giving our position away. If we saw weapons we could open fire. If not, we had the rules of war to follow where we couldn't engage unless engaged upon. By that time, one of us would probably be dead. Madness.

It meant that however we were told to act we always had to treat the locals as friendly, but sometimes we'd get the feeling that they were anything but, and rather were enemies with a hidden IED ready to blow us to smithereens. Most of them were friendly, to be fair, and were good honest people, much like the people of Northern Ireland, just getting by as best they could in difficult times. But you could never tell.

We approached Ham-El-Sidar from the west, so we wouldn't be seen by our shadows or be on a sky-line. The dogs always barked first. We could never move into any village without our presence being known.

We patrolled fifty yards away from the compound walls. We knew we couldn't take cover by the walls. The risk of a fire-fight was less than the risk of IEDs. The walls of the village could have been implanted with IEDs and the detonator pressure plate that detonated the IED one hundred yards before the actual explosion. Nobody was safe. Any one of us could have detonated the IED that killed our mate, whether they were the first or last in the patrol. Sometimes the IED was detonated not by a pressure plate but by a sensor the same as is found in homes fitted with a burglar alarm. The sensor up in the ceiling which flashes red when anyone moves was the same as those that detected our presence. You never knew who had detonated the IED that killed your mate.

Life on patrol was draining, both physically and mentally. You just never knew.

Sometimes we patrolled and used for cover the stream bed that always ran alongside the village wall. Every village needed water for personal use and for irrigation, but the Talban knew this and placed IEDs right there. Not only were they impossible to find, but they forced bacteria-filled water into the wounds. Not to mention the Taliban fighters who engaged us with rifle fire, if possible using women or children as a shield to prevent us firing back. They had no rules of engagement.

This time there were no surprises for us, only barking dogs and the smell of chapattis and fresh baked bread, chia or coffee maybe - enough to make us salivate and our bellies rumble. We entered the village compound with our Red Cross insignia prominent to show we were there in peace. We were not there to harm anyone and it was safe to show themselves. We would not ransack their homes and break everything we could. We were UK soldiers, not American soldiers.

The first man to approach us was the headman who held his right hand out to welcome us. We had a Pashtun interpreter with us who said we were there in peace and we wanted to treat any injuries or to medi-vac anyone with serious illness to Camp Bastion for hospital treatment. His face broke into a toothless grin and he said we were welcome to come into his village. He called for the women to make fresh coffee, bring bread, dates and olive oil and for the children to come out to play, before asking anyone who needed treating to come forward.

There was soon quite a queue and we knew we wouldn't make the rendezvous planned for hat night. If we had been allowed, we would be welcome to stay within the compound overnight. That way, apart from the soldiers who would be staging on guard duty, we could all have a peaceful night away from the scorpions and camel spiders. But our standing orders said otherwise.

We stayed with them all day giving medical aid and where we could we arranged a medi-vac by Chinook helicopter for later that day for those with serious illnesses and injuries. We ate their food and drank their chai and coffee, we gave the children sweets and toys, mirrors and buttons, lightweight cotton headscarves and tribally correct shemaques for the men. We even put some antibiotics into their goats. We needn't and shouldn't, but it went down well.

The day ended with all of us feeling pleased with our efforts and though the head man had offered us the space to camp inside the village walls, on reflection we decided not to. It breached all protocols and would have found us cornered in a dead-end if the Taliban came a-knocking. The one image in all our minds was the children. Like children anywhere, they had runny noses, were dirty behind their ears and loved to play. They ran all over the compound in bare feet with dogs chasing them. Adults would tell them not to shout. It was just like home except we had trainers on.

We realised that our remit couldn't be fulfilled in one day, and after a radio conference with HQ we were granted up to five days to conclude our mission. We gratefully accepted the time, set up a better than usual clinic and asked for and got a helicopter drop of drugs and freebies. After the day's work we would play games like football and rounders with the children and discuss topics with the leaders over chai and chapattis. We became firm friends. Of course, we still had to withdraw to our own camp outside the village due to the engagement rules.

One evening we had a long and very friendly but potentially explosive discussion about religion, with both the Quran and the Holy Bible read. The chances of the whole thing going belly up were too many to contemplate. And we had 'Holy Den' - our unit's bible basher from the north west of England who made us all laugh by calling tea or coffee a 'brew'. But we were glad he was with us, not only for this scenario. No-one would ever admit it publicly, but we all sought opportunities to be with him from time to time, and even the most ardent atheist found consolation from the talks they had with him but 'that never occurred'.

We discussed the foundations of Islam and Christianity and we discovered during the searches through both holy books that Abraham is a major common factor. Not only that, but the three major faiths - Islam, Christianity and Judaism - all began with Abraham. He had two sons, Ishmael and Isaac. He sent Ishmael to the east where he created Islam, and Isaac went west and created Christianity, while Abraham himself was the founding father of the Jewish faith. Anyway, that's what I think was said.

I was only listening to be polite, if truth be told.

We left that evening with new and stronger bonds between us both and we couldn't understand why we were bombing each other when all we wanted was peace and friendship.

We made our camp around eight hundred yards away, farther along the stream bed in a clearing used for keeping the goats safe, fed and watered - so it would hopefully be free from

IEDs. However, we checked the area fully. We used our metal detectors and our electronic signal barriers to prevent the use of an electronically activated detonator.

We also did something that people who haven't seen an IED would consider daft, but we called it 'on your belt buckle'. It means lying flat on your belly and looking for any unusual depressions or mounds in the ground. It sounds ludicrous but you'd be surprised how many lives and limbs it has saved.

Once cleared, we set up camp, arranged our sleeping areas with mozzie nets in place and cooking areas, and then it was time to dig our latrine. Not pleasant, but necessary in order to avoid infections. Then we sorted out who would stag on and when - and settled down into our own thoughts.

No matter how relaxed we may have looked, we were all on hyper sense, and tuned in to any unusual movement or sound. Our lives depended on our ability to be tuned in. Our mates depended on it if it was their time to be dossed down - that's what we called sleeping. We really did become as one, each one of us dependant on each other. The British Army excelled at this.

In the small hours before dawn, our sleep was broken by the high-pitched scream of jet engines with the unmistakeable whuppa whuppa sound of rotor blades. Four Apache helicopter gunships bore down on the village and opened with air to ground missiles and heavy gauge machine gun fire. The attack lasted for around one minute, but the devastation caused was like the worst horror movie you've ever watched. Like the living dead, except in this version the living were shocked into a state of numbness. There were women and children lying badly injured, some shot, some hit with fragmentation missile shrapnel, and some horrifically burnt by the incendiary component of the missiles.

The menfolk asleep after a day tending to their crops or goats, the children asleep like children anywhere and the women, some awake with babies that needed suckling... all were injured in some way. The scene was like no other the soldiers had seen, and the speed that it happened was difficult to comprehend. No sooner had our guards shouted a warning and we stood to than it was all over. The people with bodies horribly misshapen, limbs at unrecognisable angles, mouths trying to say words but saying nothing. The cluster bombs had stripped skin from bone and peppered many more with puncture wounds that still smoked because of the heat. Whatever anyone thought of as hell - this was hell on earth.

The silence after a raid isn't broken immediately. It takes some seconds before the first cry broke the silence from shock and then it rose into a crescendo as anger, pain and realisation became real. The hysteria of the children, the wails from the women and the anger of the men as they looked over at us with venom in their eyes. As far as they were concerned we had been the root of this. They thought we had softened them up, laid a trap, radioed their position to the strike force and watched with pride as they were destroyed.

But when we went to help them our bonds were soon renewed. We did what we could, and we were grateful of our standing orders otherwise we would also have been lying there with mangled and lifeless limbs.

We had withdrawn most of our medical kit with us in case the village was 'visited' by the Taliban. We were camouflaged and strategically encamped and would have been unlucky to have been seen. But we had soldiers on guard duty, and we would have been safe from any surprise attack, so we quickly made a triage and treatment area with our undamaged kit. We arranged medi-vac for over twenty casualties who needed vital treatment immediately and for further medi-vac for those needing surgery but who could wait a little while. We did what we could, and after the first triage was sorted and medi-vac'd we began to go to those who were walking wounded.

That saw us to the end of that day. It had been a long day, and one where we saw everyone as equals and we didn't hold anything back for ourselves. We administered the drugs that were needed where they were needed.

What a day, and what a blow to our hard-won bonds. We explained it was what we called a 'blue on blue' but that isn't any consolation (it never is) and when we said that the Americans had been contacted by our HQ and had offered compensation for their mistake, the air turned blue.

What we could do we did, and more. It was received with grace and that surprised us, and we wondered if we would have been as gracious if it was us that had been attacked in such a heinous way. The village elder came to us that evening with hot chai and chapattis - a sign of our firm friendship. When we said we were so sorry that the events of last night had happened, he looked at us with a sweet bewildered face and said the following while pleading with his eyes for the love born from common bonds, the bonds of Abraham:

> If the Lord my God loves me,
> And they love the Lord our God,
> Why do the Americans hate me?
> If the Lord my God loves me,
> And they hear the Lord our God,
> Why don't the Americans hear me?
> If the Lord my God loves me,
> And they pray to the same Lord our God,
> Why don't the Americans talk to me?
> If the Lord our God loves me,
> And they follow the Lord our God,
> Why wont the Americans walk with me?
> If the Lord our God loves me,
> And they love the Lord my God,
> And I love them,
> Why do the Americans persecute us?
> Why do they hate us?
> Why do they kill us?
> Why?

We had no answer. We couldn't even imagine his courage at talking to us after what had happened, but he showed us what love is. The love he had for us was so great he did what we couldn't or wouldn't do, and that was to come over to us and offer us just about all they had left - some food and some chai. What could anyone offer that was as valuable as the last of their food and their trust?

One thing the headman said to us as we left had us all choking back tears. He said 'If anyone had told us that Christians would have been so nice to us we wouldn't have believed it, but now we see that we are the same. We are all family people. People wanting a life without trouble, people who love God and want to live in peace. We aren't enemies just people. Just people'.

Futility
by Sally James

I never knew the yearning
of those who went away
to fight a war to end all wars.
I feel it now, searing, like
a bullet in the guts,
a bayonet in the heart.
A poppy uprooted.

First published 2005 in 'Tell me Grandad' by Talking Poetry.

Raindrop
by Eva Korwin-Szymanowska

Jan always looked forwards to Tuesdays. He enjoyed other days too - Wednesday lunch at the Polish Club, Sunday morning at church, and weekend visits from the grandchildren - but every Tuesday it was just him and Sophia. She understood exactly how he liked to spend those four hours that had become so precious to him.

She was his middle of three daughters, and the only one who did not have children of her own. She worked from home as a writer, so was able to commit to every Tuesday. She would arrive at exactly 11 am with a smile and a 'djien dobrez, dad' and would make immediately for the kettle. After a cup of tea and a chat, she would ask Jan if anything needed doing, and after putting the washing machine on, she would busy herself with sewing on that missing button, and dusting the ornaments on the mantelpiece - always putting them back in the wrong places. After that, he would pretend to chastise her, and they would giggle together.

Although the chores varied, the cup of tea was a routine, as was the record player. Jan and his wife, Basha, had collected many vinyl records over the years, and Sophia always selected a couple at random and played them for him whilst she pottered about his house. Jan loved to see the charcoal-black discs being removed from their sleeves, and it was always a surprise to him when the music came on as he was unable these days to recognise the coloured covers they'd been extracted from.

It was a Tuesday in summer. They had drunk their tea, and Sophia selected two long playing records. She set the first one to play, and then left the room to change her dad's bedding. Jan sat back and waited for the surprise moment when Sophia's music choice would be revealed.

The opening of Chopin's Prelude no. 15, 'Raindrops' filled his small but cosy front room. His reaction was a rush of emotion, both happy and sad, and his eyes flew to the glass-fronted display cabinet that filled the wall next to the window. 'Raindrops' had been his mother's favourite Chopin piece, and she used to hum it loudly whenever she took him and his brother, Marek, to Lasienki Park where the huge statue of

Mozart took centre stage. It was set high up, and there were about five stone steps that he and his brother would run up and down whilst mother watched on. The park also had squirrels - red ones - that would eat bits of bread straight from your hand.

Those idyllic visits were a sharp contrast to the last time he had been to Lasinski Park. It was 1944 and Jan had not been home for months. He could not risk it. The last time he had visited his mother, a woman in the upstairs flat had reported him and he had been forced to climb through the tiny kitchen window to escape.

Today he was in the park with Jerzy who was sitting behind a small brick wall. It had once been part of a summer house but had been damaged by a bomb early in the war. Jerzy was enjoying a rather strong Russian cigarette. Thankfully, Chopin had not been touched by the blast and Jan wandered over, reminiscing about his youth. He was still only 17 years old but had grown up very quickly over the last 5 years. Had he or any of his patriots known that the planned uprising would result in an apocalypse for Warsaw, they would probably not be still patrolling the park, waiting for German couriers to pass through with orders that were very valuable to the resistance. Instead, they would have been laying low, resting and preserving their lives.

He was roused by the gentle purring of a motorbike engine. He knew instantly that this was a potential courier so crouched down out of sight just inside the trees. The bikes usually came past the statue as it was a decent flat surface so as the engine noise grew, he knew that it was heading his way. He drew his pistol and watched the cycle come into view. He knew that he would be a surprise to the courier who would need time to stop and draw his weapon, so when the courier was just a few yards in front him, Jan stood up, aimed and fired.

But nothing happened.

The pistol had jammed. He tried again, but with the same result, by which time the German patrolman had drawn his pistol and taken aim at the now exposed teenager.

Jan thought this was the end. He closed his eyes and heard the shot, followed by a clatter as the cyclist and his motorcycle toppled over. Jerzy had also heard the engine and had just saved his life. Jan stood staring, shocked that he was still alive.

'Come on! Quickly!' from Jerzy woke him up. The shot would have been heard. They dragged the dead soldier from his machine, extracted the leather bag from his shoulder, and wrestled off some of his uniform before mounting the bike themselves and heading off towards the river, where they still had escape routes. The bag did indeed contain documents, and these were passed on to their superior officers.

Two weeks later, the Warsaw Uprising failed. Jan and his comrades capitulated and were taken to prisoner of war camps. He was not Jewish, and was therefore not destined for a concentration camp.

He surrendered his weapons, placing them in a huge basket that was flanked by four armed soldiers. He could keep other personal possessions, including the German courier's bag, and he was shipped off to a camp in Italy, where he survived the bullying using his wits and trading whatever he had. He sold his trousers to a guard and made himself a new pair from a blanket. At night, he put a leg of his bed in each boot so that they would not be stolen as he slept.

But one thing he would not trade was the courier's bag. Ironically, this piece of German manufacture reminded him of home, of his mother and of Chopin.

'Raindrop' had finished playing, and when Sophia came in to turn the record over, she saw that he had tears in his eyes, as he stared at the old leather bag on the bottom shelf of the display cabinet.

'Oh, dad!' said Sophia. 'Let's go for a walk in the park.'

May Day
by Eva Korwin-Szymanowska

It was the 5th of May in the year 1945. The morning sky was dull, but the air was warm when Jan climbed down from his bunk. He always got out of bed as soon as he woke up so that Ernst would not have the pleasure of tipping him out of it or soaking him and the bed in the contents of the night toilet pan. He was surprised to see that everybody else in his block was already out of the cabin and thought that he must have missed reveille altogether.

Jan walked slowly outside, just in case Ernst was waiting for him, but there was no sign of him. The yard was full of men, all moving around silently. Some looked terrified, some just looked bewildered. Jan glanced up at the sentry towers but saw no guards there, and his gaze flew quickly towards the gates. The gates! They were wide open!

Pawel came running over to him.

'Do you think it is a trick? It must be a trick!' he said. 'They want us to walk through the gates and then they are going to mow us down!'

Before Jan could answer, another man shouted: 'Back inside, everybody! It's a trick!'

Panic and shuffling erupted as men rushed off in all directions back to their huts. Jan and a few others stayed calmly outside.

They waited.

For a whole day they waited.

Those who had gone back inside stayed there. As night fell, those outside joined them, where men sat in huddles, whimpering and praying, or just sat silently.

Jan went back to his bunk, climbed up and lay down. He would wait and see what tomorrow would bring. Maybe it was a trick?

The German soldiers were not beyond such tactics, especially Ernst, who was not even liked by his fellow soldiers. Before the war he had been manservant to a mill owner who held him in little regard and fired him when he discovered that he had joined the Nazi Party. Ernst immediately joined the army and had made it to the rank of Lieutenant by the time war broke out. He played with the minds of the prisoners, chewed them up then spat them out again. He loved new arrivals - especially the young boys. He would pretend to befriend them and promised them preferential treatment, so that they trusted him enough to act as spies and slaves for him, and to indulge him where the Austrian fräuleins refused to. He became overweight and his personal hygiene left a lot to be desired.

Nobody slept that night, but as morning dawned, calm settled in Jan's bunker. A small group ventured outside, to be followed by another, and another.

Jan went out too. Everything was exactly as it had been the day before. Hunger overtook them and, with caution, several men made their way to the kitchens.

Deserted, like the sentry posts.

Scuffles broke out as they ran and snatched at any food, raw or otherwise that could be found. Jan ate along with everybody else. Then, with a few others, began to break into every store room in the camp. They found some tents and pitched them just outside the camp, still unsure and afraid of what to do.

Jan used his skills to wire lighting from the camp to the tents. Others ate then ran out of the camp, having no idea of which direction to follow or what part of Austria they were actually in.

A group of five younger boys covered a lot of ground that day and at the river caught up with a German soldier who was clearly footsore and weary. Ernst's corpulent figure had slowed him down a great deal and his fellow soldiers had refused to aid or wait for him. The five young Poles who had all suffered at his hands had no hesitation in dragging him to the centre of the river and standing on his body until they were sure that he was dead.

A few days later a group of Polish Officers arrived at the camp and were able to explain that the Americans had entered Austria and that the war was over. There was laughing, cheering, singing, crying - oh so many emotions flying round. Jan joined in for a while then sat down, mentally exhausted. What now? Where would he go?

Home Coming
by Denis Kirkham

The walk along Bolton Road was a steady climb from Albany School until you got to Fredricks ice-cream café, but each step was one step nearer to his home, Adlington in Lancashire.

Not too long ago, Adlington had felt too small for him, but right now he was hoping for all the old places and faces to be just where he had left them four years ago. Before Helmand Province and the rag-heads who tried to blow him and his mates to kingdom come by an IED.

They almost got it right, but he was the lone survivor out of six mates.

They'd been not just mates, but army mates.

Not just army mates, but Legionnaires who you'd trust with your life. But this didn't end in a story to be told and re-told over many beers in the Regiment bar. That bar was known as the 'Foyer', and the Regiment was the 2nd Regiment Legion Entrangere. All of the six comrades were 2nd Rep Legionnaires.

The blast had been expected - yet not expected.

Everyone knew the dangers of Helmand. The soldiers there put tourniquets around their thighs before leaving Camp Bastion compound. These were ready to be tightened up as soon as a blast might happen. The seconds saved could be invaluable.

The precautions were routine but fatalistic. Or was that realistic? It depended on where you were and what you were doing.

The Land Rover 110 long wheelbase with armoured base and chassis withstood the blast but still the effects were catastrophic. The original blast was enough to throw the vehicle ten feet along the track and six feet upwards. The men inside were subject to a force that left them all either suffering internal blast injuries or horrific non-survivable burns. All except for Caporal-Chef Jean Christophe.

Jean Christophe was the name given to him at Fort Aubagne, the headquarters or Quartier Vienot of the French Foreign Legion in Marseille, France.

Jean Christophe was christened Michael Robinson at St Paul's Church of England Parish Church on Railway Road in Adlington. The village had been his place of birth and location of his childhood. That was until the claustrophobia of small town Lancashire (where the men had their own place at the local pub's bars, and followed the same old rituals of working class life, birth, childhood, work, die and funeral) got to him. It never varied and was never exciting.

So he left and joined the Legion Etrangere for the excitement and the teamwork. He embraced the life of a Legionnaire: the initial joining up at Fort Aubagne, and the early training at the boot neck camp known as the 'Farm'. Then, the Marche Kepi Blanc before the award of the Kepi Blanc itself, the Legionnaire's white hat, and the culmination of the four week boot-camp before the French Pyrenees at Castelnaudry. That was where the soldiering was taught, along with French - because everything was in French. You had to learn or you would starve, and you did your learning with the occasional tough love of a dig in the ribs by the Caporals or the Chief Corporals known as Caporal-Chefs.

He loved it, quickly became well liked and marked down for Caporal school and then for the rank of Caporal itself. It was also noted that he spent his off duty time with the French speakers rather than the English speakers to help him develop better French.

He survived the blast because he was riding as vehicle commander with his body outside the vehicle observing the route and giving orders as needed.

He had been aware of a huge force pushing him through the hatch and through the air, and tumbling him along the track. But the crew were all inside the vehicle with all doors closed and all of them were literally blown apart.

He was treated by the combat medics before repatriation to France until he was fit enough for leave. One good thing came out of it though. Legionnaires wounded in battle anytime during their first five year contract were automatically given French citizenship without having to wait until their five year contract was completed.

He pondered his future as he approached Fredericks and wondered whether life in France was really any better than life within the relentless boredom of small working class towns. It was a case of six and two threes, he decided, but at least he had the sunshine.

And this complemented his decision of a two-scoop strawberry sorbet.

He entered the shop and saw one of his old school

buddies who said, 'Hi Michael, I haven't seen you for a while, been on holiday?'

Just the response he should have expected. He had been away for four years and all he got was 'Been away on holiday Michael?'

He could have screamed at this, but just said 'Been to France working, Simon. What are you doing with yourself?' only to hear 'Working at Throbshaw's shoe factory, solutioning and sticking, you know, sticking heels and soles on slippers. Love it. The smell's a bit much at times and it is only minimal pay rate but there's plenty of overtime'.

Michael screamed inside but just said 'Good for you mate' and ordered his sorbet in English which wasn't easy after four years of speaking only French.

He walked back outside and chose the 'Bottom Road' (the A6) which was the way he usually walked home when he had been returning from school.

The journey home was almost complete. He neared his house on Railway Road and wondered what reception he would get on his return.

He had sent an email to say he was coming home on leave. But was he the prodigal son or was he the pain in the bum running home when the cards fell wrongly?

He took a deep breath and tried the door. It was unlocked and he walked in. The smell got him before anything else. Chip pan fat. He almost vomited. He'd hated it then and he still hated it now.

Then he went through the door and into the living room that was decorated with the same boring wallpaper and same old bland furniture he'd known before he left.

But, unexpectedly, there was a note on the mantelpiece which read 'Make yourself at home Michael, be home at 11pm, at a darts match at the Ridgeway, fancy it?'

But after that... nothing.

He had come home after four years away. He had come home after being almost blown to kingdom come.

He had come out to reach out to his family. He'd been thinking long and hard about a treat for his parents and all he got was 'playing darts, make yourself at home'!

He looked in the fridge and saw budget boiled ham, some eggs, milk and budget margarine, a bag of limp carrots and another of spongy peppers. The larder had cornflakes, old sprouting new potatoes, crisps and carrot cake. Fantastic.

He dumped his bag on his bed in the room which had become a storage place for everything not used while he was away. It was full of boxes, bags, bin bags and rubbish.

Charming, he thought.

At least his parents could have tidied it a bit for him.

He cleared his bed and found the same sheets and bedding which probably hadn't been changed since he left. He realised how accurate his assumption was when he looked under the bed and found a pair of slippers. They were his slippers. They had not only been there forever but had actual green mould all over them.

That made his mind up.

Caporal-Chef Michel Christophe picked up his bag, went down the stairs, turned left and then through the front door.

This was the beginning of his journey back to Marseille and 'home'.

After all, the name Legionnaire meant so much to him.

The motto of the Legion ('Legio Patria Nostra') literally translates as 'Legion my Fatherland' but is known better as 'The Legion is my Family'. This is so much the case that no Legionnaire is allowed to be away from their barracks on Christmas Day. Families should be together at Christmas, so all Legionnaires and their families were at the best home they knew for Christmas.

The family he left behind - his parents - were now nothing to him. His home was the Legion.

After an incident in Afghanistan he sought home but didn't find it where he thought he had left it.

Instead, his home was now the Legion and he knew now his rehabilitation leave was to be spent with his true family. The Legion.

Brown Envelope
by Denis Kirkham

The telegram delivery man rode his bicycle along the leafy lanes of Rivington whistling as he went along, up short hills and down the other side. He cycled with the sun warming his face and the birds singing in the early morning mist, while newly hatched damsel flies flew precariously along the water's edge of the reservoir that served the homes in nearby Adlington. The brown envelopes in his bag were not good news for most, but for others they brought relief that their man was not dead but a prisoner until hostilities ceased. They contained an address for the Red Cross that sent parcels to the prisoners as often as the enemy allowed and would also contain 'letters from the home-front'.

The bicycle slowed down naturally near to the Bay Horse pub at the top of Babylon Lane. This was where his next telegram was to be personally handed over. This always meant the contents were very bad news, the worse news. He knew this as he had been the recipient of one such telegram himself when his only child - a son as strong as an ox who wanted no more than to follow his father into the Royal Mail - had lost his life when he parachuted onto enemy soil. The enemy were waiting for them and killed fifty six soldiers that night, but he died bravely, the telegram told him. And this was later said when he received a letter from his commanding officer.

The telegram was addressed to a cottage near the top of Babylon Lane - a pretty home with ivy creeping up its front, with brightly coloured flowers in the garden and the door knocker well polished. He stood himself tall and straightened his hat before he used the door knocker to make the inhabitants aware of his presence. The door was opened by a portly lady of middle age who collapsed into his arms when she saw the brown envelope. She shook and cried loud enough for her neighbours to open their doors, run over to her and help her inside.

The telegram man stood in a lovely living room. Displayed were pictures of two sons (he presumed) and one of a man who could have been the husband and father of the younger men. All were standing tall in army uniform and looked very proud of who they were and where they were.

One of the neighbours helped the woman to sign for the telegram before motioning him into the kitchen where there was a kettle always on the boil. She made him tea.

The woman was totally bereft.

The neighbour making the tea told him that the oldest soldier in the photograph was the woman's husband. He had been killed at Ypres. The two younger soldiers were her sons, one of whom had been killed at Dunkirk during the evacuation of the troops retreating from France. She only had one other son, and no daughters or other family members.

It was obvious from her grief that the brown envelope contained the news that every family dreaded. It was a letter that told of a loss and not imprisonment. Her youngest son had been killed in Holland, at a bridge near Arnhem, and died bravely.

She had no illusion that every telegram said the same. She had two other telegrams under her bed in a shoe box, along with the usual letter from their commanding officers.

She had no-one to welcome home. Whatever peace would mean would never reach her. She was a widow without family. Where would she go to now at Christmas, where would she go to on Mothers Day or Easter? As a family they had trekked to the top of Rivington Pike with a cross made by the local church at Rivington village. The cross would be placed in the ground before a short service, then a bun-fight of home-made sandwiches and fancy buns before home and a meal which compared only to Christmas Day in its opulence. No more would she wash shirts every Monday, or iron them on Tuesday, looking lovingly at her family who had fallen asleep after a Sunday dinner of roast beef and the usual trimmings. Her life was no more life but was years of loneliness until God called her home.

She hoped it wouldn't be a long wait.

The Officer
by Denis Kirkham

The corporal stood his section to attention as the officer in pristine uniform strode with disdain along the section. He reprimanded every man about his uniform - loose puttees, dirty boots or scruffy battledress. He was just out of Sandhurst and less than a week ago had been playing polo at Hickstead with quails' eggs and smoked salmon for afternoon tea. He was now striding along the line on the morning of the 15th July 1916. The section of trench he had been allocated to was like any other - rough and not like the examples shown at Sandhurst.

The men were downbeat and seemed not to care about rank or dress, which was quite the opposite of what he had been told to expect. The lower ranks were supposed to be gracious to officers, to immediately stand to when he spoke to them and always to have their uniform to the book. He discovered that there was some apathy among the ranks, as if they were there but not there, almost purposefully. They were bodies with no souls, as if life had been taken from them.

Laziness, he called it, and ordered all men, NCOs included, to be inspected at 0700 hrs tomorrow - the 16th of July 1916. This was in preparation for the walkover to the Jerry lines at 0730 hrs. A tidy well-presented soldier was an effective soldier, and until then he would retire to his dugout where his batman would serve tea and then prepare his uniform for the morning. He had been told by his predecessor at afternoon changeover that dinner was to be young chicken and roast vegetables. He had been presented with hard boiled eggs and mashed potatoes followed by a slice of duff and custard. He had reprimanded his batman for being so lax with his cooking until he saw the faces of the other three officers in the dugout who had placed bets that he would be killed or have 'Gone West' by now. They knew they were already dead except death hadn't yet happened. They knew why the officers names were only written on a blackboard with chalk, including their own.

The officer was woken by his batman at 0600 hrs though he hadn't slept at all due to the infernal noise from the guns. The bed was uncomfortable too - the blankets were filthy and the mattress was straw in a hessian cover. He had no doubts about the hygiene of it. But still his batman was cleaning his boots and laying his uniform out to retain the creases in the trousers. He felt that the other officers were of doubtful military heritage, unlike himself. He had an impeccable military background which allowed his father to pull strings and have him offered a commission at Sandhurst before his 18th birthday. And here he was at 19 years old - a Lieutenant in the Regiment of Surrey Rifles and with a future of military stardom before him.

His men were aged from sixteen to thirty seven years of age. Some were better than others, his predecessor had told him, but all were willing to go over the top with him to a glorious day of victory. His NCOs were men of distinction to be trusted: battle hardened and staunch under fire. The trench had been readied with stronger fire steps to make the soldiers able to mount the ladders leading to no mans land. The men would have to carry loads with them - barbed wire, extra ammunition and food. These loads were to be their downfall, it transpired, as they slowed them down so much they became cannon fodder.

The officer strode along the line at 0630 hrs and rattled off orders of discipline to his sergeant. They related to dress, dull buttons, ill fitting tunics, and lack of energy when standing to. All these were attributes Sandhurst had warned him about that needed to be nipped in the bud and rewarded with extra duties or loss of leave. He strode along like some tin-pot headcase as some of the men called him and they weren't worried about his disciplinary awards as they all knew he would 'Go West' in an hour or so. They just stood to and remained passive as he spoke to them.

He came to the youngest soldier of his section who he found shivering with fear with tears in his eyes. He clearly was wondering what death would feel like as he couldn't stop himself from repeating Psalm 23, even when the officer said he would have him court marshalled if he saw any lack of courage from him. The young soldier was fourteen, not sixteen as he had told the recruiting officer, but he had wanted to be in the army for the victory of the Empire. He was sweating pink, literally blood, as his blood pressure rose to such an extent that the capillary blood vessels in his skin leaked blood. He just wanted 0730 hrs to come and for him to be killed and for his suffering to be over.

The Officer called 'Stand To' at 0725 hrs and his men stood manfully to the fire step ready to go over the top. He himself stood first man and watched his men ready to walk over no mans land to have tea in the Jerry lines with him and for him to be awarded his first gong of many.

The artillery stopped and the barrage over, the day was clear and quite pleasant. A small sparrow hopped along the trench picking at crumbs. This seemed quite bizarre in the circumstances and reminded those who still believed in God about the gospel reading that taught them that the sparrow didn't worry about food so they shouldn't worry about their lives. They believed that God forbade them to worry about the next few hours, so they jutted their jaws out and stiffened their backs ready for the whistle taking them to glory - one way or the other.

The officer blew his whistle and cried 'For Country and Empire' as he climbed the fire step and mounted the parapet and strode towards the opposite lines. Having a blindingly ridiculous belief in victory, he was incensed to see some of his men already dropping to their knees to have a rest from carrying their loads.

The first bullet hit him in his right shoulder and spun him round 360 degrees. He was confused when he saw blood staining his new tunic, but he was made of Sandhurst training and didn't break stride and held the flag aloft. It was a flag that had been issued to him to help his men orientate themselves to his position.

The second bullet hit him in his left thigh shattering the bone and causing him fall to the ground, but he tried manfully to crawl along the line he had been allocated with his one functioning leg and arm raised to show the small flag, now blood stained.

He saw many men falling to clear stoppages in their rifles or to catch their breath so he called at them to 'Tally Ho' and maintain their forward line. It was then when the third bullet hit him in his chest. He felt no pain, and with eyes searching the sky he fell dead.

His batman who had been told to prepare him a nice tea to bring along the lines after the first wave of victory, watched with horror at the sight of men being blown, ripped or torn limb from limb, and from life itself. He shook and cried, visibly bereft at the slaughter and the Surrey Rifles' demise. Stretcher bearers came along the trench to do their best for the injured and ignore the pleas of the dying, and he offered himself to help. They gave him an armband, and when a stretcher bearer came along without a partner they allocated him to become one of a two-man stretcher bearer party.

The death cries lasted all day until darkness fell, when a strange eerie silence befell the line and stretcher bearers were allowed a cease fire to reach the injured men. They needed to bring them back to the trench and clearing stations before getting them to a field hospital.

The fourteen year old lad was found with both legs shot away but was still alive.

The officer was found dead and was left where he lay.

The sergeant was found with one wound that had killed him outright.

Their disciplinary infringements were lost with them as four new officers strode along the trench that night giving their own thoughts on the laziness and lack of backbone shown by the Surrey Rifles. The boasted that their men, the Wiltshires, would be better by far and told the stretcher bearers to show some respect to them and to salute as they passed by. They were excited by the smell of cordite and the number of bullet cases in the trench. And by the detritus of soldiers lying where they were ready to be claimed by the owner when they returned from the new front line, full of song and ready for the next 'big push'.

The officer, the fourteen year old lad and the sergeant were all buried together. The batman was detailed to a new officer and was killed when he was told to go forward to seek identification tags from the fallen.

Many years later, during World War Two, Winston Churchill said this: 'Perish in the common ruin rather than fail or falter in your duty'.

The little sparrow hopped along the trench the following morning, not caring about his future as the Empire and the Hun began a new morning of killing.

Preparing for Christmas, 1944
by Delia Southern

Remember ladies, that the secret of a successful Christmas despite rationing is to start preparations early.

I know that you will have been putting away small amounts of necessary foodstuffs all year, but look out for different helpful recipes to share with your friends and neighbours. We are told by the government to 'eat more spuds' and it is true that potatoes par-boiled and then roasted with a little dripping or lard are a tasty way of stretching the dinner. I have seen most ingenious recipes for custard and 'cream' for trifles, and new ways of using garden and hedgerow fruits in Christmas cakes and for mince pie fillings. If you send a stamped addressed envelope, this magazine will be happy to share them with you.

Last year, I was thrilled to receive from a clever friend a packet of steel wool for cleaning my saucepans, while from another a tin of custard powder was very gratefully received.

This year, I'm making beauty gifts - not the luxury preparations of pre-war, but more mundane toiletries that, because of scarcity, are precious now.

I found, hiding away in an old suitcase, a really big bottle of bath salts. I intend to make little bags from scraps of organdie to wrap some small jars. Cold cream goes down well with my land-girl friends whose hands suffer and I have managed to find a few bars of soap, although these have cost soap-coupons.

Of course, all gifts must be suitable for the recipient. A small girl I know was delighted to receive a small doll, until she undid the ribbon 'sash' and it fell into its component parts of a dish mop, a duster and a couple of pegs.

My mother has found some coloured cellophane and used her sweet ration to buy dolly mixtures to fill cellophane dorothy bags for her grandchildren. She has hung the bags on whitewashed twigs in a vase and the result is quite magical.

One good thing the war has done, you know; it's made us quite thrilled to receive the humblest of gifts and we really do value things because of the thought behind them and the effort they entailed - rather than for their splendour!

At Christmas, we will remember those who have lost so much and will be grateful for what we have. To know that you have enough is to be rich.

Daphne Alone
by Lesley Atherton

Even Daphne's skirt, a heavy, sensible tweed - rusty brown, unpatterned, and ending just two inches below her equally heavy and sensible knees - was no match for weather such as this. In common with most of her countrywomen, she resorted to an ankle-length heavy waxed coat when leaving the house, but when the wind moved from playful to aggressive like an out-of-control puppy who has little idea of its own power and strength - when the gales experimented with moving around what had previously seemed immoveable... that was when the women of Daphne's acquaintance resorted to a heavy contrivance of ropes draped and tied round their bodies.

For, without such ropes, Jean, her neighbour of two miles distant had suffered. She'd neglected to secure her clothing, just the once, and was inelegantly blown into Daphne's neighbouring field, her diaphanous coat acting as a parachute, or rather as a sail which propelled her perilously close to the edge of the deep and rocky riverbank.

It was an expensive lesson to be learned as Jean's path had led her to demolish more than one fence, and had also led to what looked to be a long-ish hospital stay owing to multiple breaks, surface wounds and bruises.

That was why Daphne was out in this weather. Her sheep weren't brought in for the winter. She couldn't afford such an extravagance, so she had to focus her not inadequate energies on keeping safe and intact what flock she still had.

So, with the men being gone for the last three years, and with only the too young, too old and too incapable remaining, there was nothing for it but for Daphne to mend her own fences.

With hammer and nails in her coat's capacious pockets and with a saw tied with string and slung around her back; with dinky feet encased in her husband's galoshes (padded with three thick pairs of socks); and with her hand-knitted woollen balaclava itching her already red and chapped face, Daphne began the trudge to the first fence repair. Behind her strong but weary frame she dragged a sledge-like contraption she'd roughly fashioned as a means of carrying the larger of the loads she needed to haul. She began to tug and pull and the rope lessened the wood load which thudded heavily behind her.

Not for the first time that day, Daphne had wished there

was no war, there was no compulsory conscription and there was no forced separation of families. She wished that Gerald, her husband of eight years, had been able to stay at home. And she wished he would do his bit around the farm and stop jobs such as this one from being her sole responsibility. But, as happened every time young Daphne (who was only 26) allowed her mind to raise such thoughts, she forced them away with vehemence.

One must not allow one's thoughts to overtake sensibility. Crying over spilt milk. No. There was no point at all allowing one's self to brood. One simply must 'get on with it' when one felt weak or threatened. Now was such a time - skies were darkening already with the onset of early twilight.

Daphne knew how much more afraid she'd be if she was living in one of the many miserable bomb-threatened towns or cities, but, still, there might be some joy to be had. There might be friends for comfort during the blackouts and in the air raid shelters too.

Here there was only Jean. Both women had been left alone in the most remote of sheep farming communities. And up here there were no land girls. No support. It was just Daphne and Jean.

It was Daphne who had discovered Jean's battered and broken body. It appeared a corpse at first, and Daphne had been greatly relieved when Jean began to cough. Daphne had loaded Jean onto her roap-pulled sledge contraption, and rushed back to the village's post office to summon the doctor.

And now she was left to fix the damage.

Her hands were raw and almost purple with cold and strain by the time she arrived at the first gate. Midst the hammering and sawing, Daphne allowed herself a little self-indulgence - a wandering mind. And there was so much to think of - the absence of her husband, mainly, but in recent times another thought had become more prominent - the fact that the pair of them had not yet produced children.

At times like this it was almost as if she had nostalgia for a time and life that she had never personally known. Anemoia, the term was. She knew it because she'd encountered it in the village's library.

She'd spent a lot of time there when her husband first left. Quite a few of the village ladies did the same - teaching themselves about life and the world, taking comfort in the company of others, talking of the life they now had, and the life they missed.

They talked of the days when their husbands received the call-up papers.

And they talked of the progress of the fighting, the sounds of the telegram boys, the little evacuees who'd just appeared in the village, and the contents of their husbands' regular but stilted letters home. They talked of unravelling old sweaters to re-knit into more useable clothing, and how to cope without hosiery.

There was an unplanned and unexpected small crop of barley in the corner near where Daphne was working. She would have to protect that from the sheep. But it could wait.

As Daphne's self-indulgent thoughts slowed, she realised that she'd mended the fence, and that the rain which had been sprinkling onto her waterproof layers and puddling around her feet and inside her overly capacious galoshes - the rain had stopped, and the sky had darkened. Her eyes struggled in this kind of light, but she had to get back to the farm before it darkened entirely.

Her small, chapped and frozen hands replaced the spare wood onto her sledge and she began the trudge back to her home. Thighs and calves tingled numbly with the cold and it was just as well, as her aching and pained leg muscles needed the numbness to dull the pain.

She had no watch, but she knew it was late by the time she returned home, wishing, not for the first time, that there was someone waiting.

Daphne immediately made her way to the kitchen and the warmth of the range. Stoking it up once again, she began to relax a little. The casserole warming inside her oven should be almost ready.

She got up and ladled herself a good portion of butter beans, potato, green onion tops and gravy browning. She ate. Nothing was ever quite enough.

The house was dark and silent. No candles. No wireless.

She glanced at the kitchen wall clock as she laid down her spoon after the meagre meal. Half past six. Bedtime.

And tomorrow was another day.

Last Post
by Sally James

When his letter came, she kissed it before opening - to taste him on the envelope where his lips had sealed. She traced her fingers where he had written, imagined them soiled with mud, but gentle, ever so gentle, when he was writing her name.

She opened it and read the first few lines. How he was missing her, had her photograph in his pocket and how the other lads envied him. He said how cold it was most of the time and how he wished she could warm him.

Then there was a funny scrawl as if his pencil had slipped. Sorry, he had written, but there was such a crack just then like lightening and thunder and it lit up the sky and all the lads' faces.

How I wish it were just that, sweetheart. Remember the thunderstorm and how we sheltered in that old barn over the fields?

Sometimes, he wrote, when the smoke clears I look at the sky and imagine you looking at the same moon as I do, not hazy with mist like it is here, but clear and bright with a halo around it.

There is a star just below it at the moment. It has been there all week. I think it is Venus. It is shining ever so brightly. I imagine it is you.

Anyway, he ended, I will have to go now. Soon it will be my watch. I should be sleeping really but I can't stop thinking of you. Thanks for the socks by the way, I see Aunt Maud is still knitting away like there is no tomorrow.

I really must go now, sweetheart, or the sergeant will have my guts for garters.

Remember that I love you, my darling, and my heart is yours for always.

Your ever-loving husband and true love Walter. xxxxx

She folded the letter, placed it back in the envelope, wiped away her tears and placed it on the mantelpiece next to the telegram from the war office.

In the Trench
by Delia Southern

'Sergeant Higgins reporting, Captain Sir, and this is all that's left of the Third.'

'Lieutenant Phillips is dead?'

'Yes, sir, he will be by now. He was badly injured by a sniper yesterday and we have been under fire ever since until just before we left. We wanted to get him out then, but he said that he was too bad and he'd be more use playing Horatius at the bridge when the Germans' big push came in the next few minutes. He said we would be more use to you alive than dead in the next ten minutes if we stayed. We didn't want to leave him, but he said it was an order and we had to go. Then the guns stopped and he said 'The Assyrians came down like wolves on the fold. Off you go, boys!' and we had to go. I don't quite get what he meant. Maybe you do, Sir?'

'Well, yes I do. But you look all in; you did well to get here. When did you last eat or sleep?'

'We've had no food for two days, since the camp kitchen got blown up, along with the rest of the men at that end of the trench. Sleep - I don't rightly know - I can't remember that far back.'

'You can rest a bit and have a bite and then we will send you back with the supply truck to recover properly. I am really sorry about Phillips, but you can be proud of him.'

War: The Fallen: Honoured and Spurned
by Peter Hull.

Martha stood at the front door of her small, terraced house, as she watched John in his uniform walk proudly up the street. Three times he turned round and waved till he neared the corner and he gave her a final cheerful wave. Then, typical of John, there was just his hand and then with a thumbs up, he was gone.

She hesitated on the step before going back into the house. He had gone, but the real dark cloud was that he had been on embarkation leave. That was all he could say, but she was sure he would soon be on his way to France - and the war.

She could not let her thoughts run wild but the uncertainty… too many people she knew had received one of those little yellow envelopes telling them of their loss - a husband, a son, a brother, the father of young children.

Martha was strong and told herself she had to be brave and positive. Her strength came from a life which had never been easy. Her father had walked out when she was only six, leaving her mother devastated. From then on she just lost all interest in life and in her daughter. So Martha grew up a lonely child of a child living in near-poverty.

On leaving school she found work in one of the local mills and things began to look up as she made friends and her wage helped to alleviate a little of the poverty of her childhood.

When Martha met Harry things seemed even better. She gradually realised that he was a charmer and a rather shallow character and as time went on her doubts grew in spite of her love. Then she felt the emotion of her love and his deceit - 'I promise I'll marry you' and then she fell pregnant.

When there was no doubt of her state, Harry's promise of marriage was forgotten and he vanished from the scene. Martha was again on her own. As expected, her mother gave her no support and for the first of many times she was called 'A Fallen Woman'.

This always cut her to the quick. She had given in to Harry out of her love for him, and he had acted out of selfishness and deceit, then abandoned her and his child. But Martha's strength came through and she managed to earn a living and bring up John with great love and devotion.

Most people accepted her and John, and this she supposed was for different reasons. Some knew they should not judge, and others recognised their own frailty, but there were always the self-righteous ever ready to dub Martha the 'Fallen Woman'.

One of the people who supported her the most was the Reverend Jackson, the local vicar. One afternoon when they were chatting over a cup of tea he told her in strict confidence that his mum had never married and she had also been called a 'Fallen Woman'.

I've turned out alright,' he smiled, 'and I'm sure your John will too'.

And so he did. When John left school he found work in a local hardware shop until he joined the army and left Martha and home for the first time.

All these thoughts went through Martha's head that day John went off to war. During the days that followed, her thoughts oscillated - sometimes she felt John would be fine and certain to return home safely and at other times she feared the worst.

Then her fears were realised. A loud knock on the door and the telegram boy, his face concerned and embarrassed, handed over the little yellow envelope.

'Sorry missus - I hope it isn't.'

And then he was gone.

Martha stood there, stunned. Drained. She slowly closed the door but was unable to move. Finally, clutching the envelope tightly in her hand, and supporting herself on the wall, she dragged herself back to her chair in front of the fire.

It took an age before she slowly and deliberately opened the envelope and then a further age before she unfolded the small sheet of paper, as if this might save her from what she knew was inside.

Her hands were shaking uncontrollably as she read.

'We regret to inform you...'

The rest was a blur, but there was no need to read on.

The tears coursed down her cheeks. Her John was gone and then she realised that once again she was on her own and then the through suddenly struck Martha - it must have been a week ago now when she had been aware of John's presence like she had never felt it before. She had tried to dismiss it as her imagination, but still it returned and then she had noticed her dog. When these thoughts came upon Martha, Bessie's ears pricked up and she sat up alert.

Friends and neighbours gave her what support they

could but it did little to assuage her grief. There was not even the finality of a funeral to give some closure. Just sheer emptiness.

Her grief came to a head each evening as she sat in her darkened kitchen, her tea waiting unappetisingly on the table. Tears ran silently down her cheeks and at times she sobbed aloud as she could no longer control her grief. Bessie, with the sense many animals have, would place her head on Martha's knees, looking up into her face, as she sat there in silent desolation.

It was about three weeks after receiving the news as Martha silently grieved that she felt a presence. Opening her eyes, there he was kneeling beside her, the pressure of his hands on hers. It was not the feel of a living person but her hands were being held tightly by John.

What struck Martha was that his face was radiant and he confirmed this.

'Mam, I am sorry you are so sad, but I am safe and I am happy. Try not to worry. But there is some good news: Ellen is going to have a baby and it's a boy - my son and your grandson. She is a 'Fallen Woman' too, he smiled.

Martha managed to force a smile in reply as, in spite of the good news, her grief was overwhelming.

'A grandson to remind me of you and a son for Ellen - a reminder for her.'

'She's not sure yet, but you can tell her, mam, and ask her please to call him John - my son'

They sat there in silence for a few minutes and she felt a squeeze on her hands. John whispered.

'I'm going now, mam. I too am one of the fallen,' and with his cheeky grin, he was gone.

Room For One More
by Neville Southern

Lying in bed was no longer a perfect expectant experience, but Connie went to bed early as usual. After all, she lived alone in the house, with her husband listed as 'missing in action' and the nightly bombing raid would bring its interruption soon enough. Her brain was restless and she knew that she could not get the sleep she needed without the help of a sleeping pill, so she risked taking one.

She slept fitfully as a nightmare developed.

She found herself looking out of her bedroom window. The suburban street looked particularly dark and gloomy in the absence of streetlights or lights from houses - all because of the omnipresent blackout curtains.

She could make out a gleaming black horse-drawn hearse, but could see no coffin or flowers inside. Instead, the hearse was packed with laughing, waving people. The driver looked up at her, and Connie momentarily thought that he resembled her husband.

'There's room for one more,' he said, his voice strangely familiar. She drew the curtains together and jumped back into bed, pulling the quilt over her head.

Inevitably, the sirens woke her. Still dozy because of the pill, she pulled on the clothes that she had laid out and made her way towards the air-raid shelter in the cellar of the local chapel. All the usual occupants must already be there before her, she thought as she heard the babble from within.

The air-raid warden at the entrance said 'There's room for one more' - and, as he spoke, his face reminded her immediately of the driver of the hearse in her dream.

'No,' she said quickly, 'I'll try round the corner'.

'Please yourself,' said the warden in a surly tone, 'You can't please some people,' as he pulled the iron door to with a clang.

Connie ran down the street, but had scarcely reached the corner when a tremendous blast hit her, bowling her over, and the ground shook beneath her as she sprawled. A huge bomb had scored a direct hit on the chapel.

There were no survivors.

Isabel's Kitchen
by Delia Southern

The kitchen was old even for the 1940s. Circumstances had meant that there had been no money to modernise it, so it looked very much as it had when Isabel's great-aunt and uncle had built it in 1890.

The floor was flagged with rag rugs. A large airing rack hung from the ceiling. The sink was deep, square and ceramic, with a wooden draining board. The large range was gas and was nowhere near as safe as a modern one.

The kitchen was always draughty because of the number of doors opening off it. Apart from the not very well-fitting back door that opened onto the yard outside, there was the door into the living room, a broom cupboard and two doors into pantries with large stone slabs. They faced north and were always cold even in summer - as they should be.

Looking round, one could tell who lived in the house. Over the sink was the large kitchen window. Next to the window hung a strop and a small shaving mirror, with a towel below and a shaving mug on the window sill, holding an old, but still good, ivory and badger-hair shaving brush. On the chair next to the broom cupboard sat a doll, temporarily forgotten by her owner. On the airing rack were clothes, carefully ironed, that belonged to an old man, a woman and a little girl.

Isabel was washing up and worrying about food again. It was not easy to keep a family fed in war-time, especially when her father had standards that forbade him, and Isabel, of course, to consider any source that was even slightly dubious, much less black-market. Other women queued, but Isabel had been the breadwinner since her father had been laid off in 1931. Her brother had joined the RAF straight from university. Isabel had no spare time; as well as working full-time she was a fire-watcher three nights a week.

'I knew Dad wouldn't queue,' she told herself, 'so why am I fretting about it now?' She was not an expert cook as her mother had been, because her mother would never let her help in the kitchen. This was owing to the fact she had felt guilty that Isabel had to work so hard to keep them all. Isabel missed her mother, not because of the extra work but because she was so lonely without her. She loved her little daughter, but no small child could provide the companionship that the two women had enjoyed through all the hardships of the last 14 years.

She wiped her hands on the thin linen towel.

Now it seemed that the war was almost over and food might be more plentiful soon, but the powers-that-be were making no firm promises and she had to provide some sort of celebration for her daughter's fifth birthday on the 14th May, which was only a week away.

All that fruit in the garden, but none of it ripe yet. The sugar needed to be kept for jamming as her jam was one of the few things she could swap for necessities.

'Of course,' she sighed with relief, 'I'll swap that last pot of raspberry for four eggs and let her have Sheila and Pat for tea. I'll make egg nests with three of the eggs and a small cake with candles on the top with the other one. That's settled'.

Satisfied, she turned out the single dim light bulb and went through to the living room, where there was a fire and music from the radio her father had made.

Publisher and Other Publications

Scott Martin Productions came into being in 2018 with their first ten titles - two anthologies, two novelettes, four short story collections, one book of children's poems and one full length novel. 2019 sees eight more confirmed publications, with others yet to be announced.

We are what I like to call a community publisher, which is the entire opposite to a vanity publisher. We will publish work we believe to be good and which deserves to be made accessible to the general public, especially work by beginning writers and writing groups - and works which explore the unfashionable genres we love - short stories and short novels.

We charge nothing for our publishing services. Like the author, we take royalties on sales, so it is to everyone's advantage to have a great book and to promote it so it sells. Please feel free to contact us on scottmartinproductions@gmail.com. Hope to hear from you soon.

2018 titles

'Time' and '…and Tide' are the first two titles published by Write You Are, a writing group based in Horwich, Lancashire. They are both anthologies of wonderfully rich and diverse short prose and poetry by an incredibly talented bunch of writers.

'Changes' and 'Divine Intervention' are two novelettes by Lesley Atherton. The first is the tale of illness, change, adoption, family and discovery, while the second is narrated by God, the ultimate in omniscient narrators and tells the story of twins - one good, and the other evil.

'Masked' is a novel by Pat Laurie which explores intertwined families and sexual discovery in 1960s England, all set against a background of nursing.

'The Wasamaroo' by Sally James takes our publishing in an entirely different direction, being a book of children's poems and nonsense rhymes - all of which have been tried and tested on relatives of the author for many years.

The other four titles are the first four volumes in the 'Can't Sleep, Won't Sleep: Tales for Travellers' series of short stories and flash fiction by Lesley Atherton.

Extracts of all these books are available on http://www.scottmartinproductions.com, to whet your appetite before purchasing, either on Kindle or paperback.

2019 titles (confirmed)

Alongside 'Wartime Tales' will be published 'Survival' - another anthology of short stories on a specific theme. 2019 will also see three novels by Lesley Atherton. The first, 'Past Present Tense' is a story of old age, of hoarding and of desperation, in which (ultimately) all the characters get their happy endings. 'Walking with Eve' tells the tale of two women brought together by their bigamous shared husband. They seek revenge and grow closer in the process. 'No Matter What' is a story of the most positive of people - who believes that all will be well 'no matter what'.

In addition to these titles, we will also be publishing 'Another Time' - the third anthology by Write You Are - and the fifth volume of short stories in the 'Can't Sleep, Won't Sleep' series by Lesley Atherton, as well as 'Melissa and the Mobility Scooter' - a book of children's stories for happy bedtimes.

A large number of other titles are also under consideration, but do not yet have release dates so do check out our website for more information. http://www.scottmartinproductions.com.

Printed in Great Britain
by Amazon